Also by Susan Dunlap

AN EQUAL OPPORTUNITY DEATH

A Mystery By

SUSAN DUNLAP

A DELL BOOK

Published by
Dell Publishing
a division of
Bantam Doubleday Dell Publishing Group, Inc.
1540 Broadway
New York, New York 10036

This is a work of fiction. Any reference to actual people or places is purely coincidental.

ISBN: 0-440-21566-8

Printed in the United States of America

Published simultaneously in Canada

October 1994

10 9 8 7 6 5 4 3 2 1

RAD

For Susie, Namasté

CHAPTER

1

It was cold in my parlor that morning, the day Frank Goulet died. I didn't realize how long it took to warm the room, with only the fireplace for heat.

Normally I didn't have time to notice the cold. I downed my coffee as I raced between the bedroom, the kitchen, and the bath, grabbing clothes and putting on make-up, always almost late for work. Lateness is frowned upon by Pacific Gas and Electric, the local utility company and my employer. Occasionally, I had gotten up this early on a weekend, but that had been in summer, or autumn. But now it was March, it was raining, and the room was freezing.

This was my first self-proclaimed holiday. I had to get up early enough to call in sick. And having committed myself to that lie, I couldn't be seen outside, in perfect health, indeed, in better spirits than if I had been at work—trudging up the endless wooden staircases that led to endless charming wooden houses nestled in the redwoods along the Russian River. Reading electricity meters endlessly.

I started to Thompson's Grocery for the newspaper, then realized I couldn't go there. The grocery was right in Henderson, and Joe and Elsa Thompson saw me every day, often two to three times a day, as I rushed in for essentials or an emergency chocolate bar.

I felt like a spy avoiding the omnipresent eyes of PG&E. Playing out the fantasy, I drove twelve miles to an anonymous truck stop on Route 101, the main north-south freeway between San Francisco and the Oregon border, to buy my paper.

There, having breakfast in a booth twenty feet from the cash register, were two people from town —Madge Oombs, who ran an antique store of sorts, and Skip Bollo, the realtor who sold me my house. An odd couple. Madge was a sturdy, no-nonsense, Henderson-born woman who had created a surprisingly decent business out of other people's discards. She had outlived one husband and outlasted another, and had the lowest electric usage level of anyone on my route. Skip Bollo was middle-aged, comfortably tweedy, and gay.

Normally I would trot over for a few words and, with luck, sate my curiosity. But today, I pulled up the hood of my slicker, which sent a stream of water down my back, and hurried out.

Shielded from view by the steady rain, I drove home. Then, with a mound of scrambled eggs, a pot of coffee, and my newspaper in front of me, I sat by the inadequate fire, feeling deliciously illicit.

The furniture came with the house—heavy floral pieces from the fifties that belonged in pine-panelled rooms. I adjusted the overstuffed reading chair and its ottoman so that my feet were nearly in the fire, refilled my coffee cup, and started through the paper.

I read the articles about the Russian River area, savoring the crime and scandal. There was another foul-up in the construction of the sewer system that was already two years and five million dollars over estimate. The pipes didn't fit together! And burglaries. In summer the Russian River provided San Franciscans with a rustic resort in the redwoods that was only two hours away, with fishing and swimming, or a short drive over to the Pacific Ocean. In winter their untended houses were the bread and butter of local burglars. Housebreaking was almost as big a business as marijuana. Burglaries never even made the paper. But this year a professor had brought ten Chinese religious plates to his house and within a week they were gone. That had garnered the attention of the state police, caused comments from every city and county official, and filled news space for the past two months. Today's column pondered whether the crime had signaled the entry of outside forces into the area, or if it had merely been a bonanza for local thieves.

By eleven o'clock, the paper discarded, the coffeepot empty, and the parlor still nowhere near warm, I began to tire of the game of hooky. I considered driving to the city—to San Francisco. I still had plenty of friends there. But, of course, they would be at work. I had friends here, too, whom I couldn't see today. I had chores that had been put off for days, weeks, ever since I bought the house last year. But an illicit sick day couldn't be demeaned by work.

A steady rain hit the windows, creating a transparent curtain between the house and the redwoods beyond. Outside, the ground was soft from the constant rainfall of the last three months. There had been landslides, but not bad ones. The

Russian River was filling; there was no question but that it would flood.

I carried the breakfast dishes through the dining room to the kitchen, put them in the sink, and stared out the window at the water trailing down the hillside. The bedroom was off the kitchen, the farthest point from the fireplace. It never got warm in there. When I thought about sitting on my bed and writing letters, I realized I was procrastinating. And what I was avoiding was going to see Frank Goulet.

Leaving the dishes to soak, I grabbed my yellow slicker and so camouflaged, crept down the steps (fifty-two in all) from the house. The steps formed a sloping Z from the house to the garage. At the top corner a growing torrent of water flowed over the landing, forcing me to hang on to the none-too-sturdy railing (fixing it was a longstanding item on my list of chores). Only fairly wet, I made it to the garage and climbed into my pickup truck.

The river was high, but still six to eight feet below flood stage. I crossed the old bridge and drove down the macadam past the canoe rental that Paul and Patsy Fernandez managed. In summer, when the tourists filled every rented room and camped on the river benches, Paul and Patsy were busy until long after sunset. But now the boats were up and the building looked deserted, except for a dim light in the back. Only those of us who knew them well were aware they were living in the storeroom.

Businesses were mixed in with guest houses along South Bank Road, and Frank's Place sat back from the road—a one-story, white, shingle structure raised five feet above street level and overlooking the river. The guest houses on either side were strictly summer operations, now closed, with furniture safe on the second floor. Their owners wouldn't come back to Henderson till after the flooding, in time to wash out the mud.

Frank's Place looked closed too, but I knew that a knock would get me inside. I pulled the pickup around back, got out and peeked through the glass in the door. The interior of Frank's Place was nothing like its outside. It was cozy, panelled (like most older buildings along the river), with gilt-framed landscapes on the walls. I could see the bar, and behind it, I spotted Frank.

I knocked.

Frank pushed open the door. "Come in, Veronica."

"Vejay."

He shrugged. "Very well, Vejay, but it is a bit adolescent to change your name. And Veronica is a lovely name. It has history. Vejay is just . . "

"Adolescent?" I laughed and climbed up on the bar stool, the rainboots heavy on my feet. Looking at Frank Goulet as he walked behind the bar, it was still clear what had attracted me and every other new woman in Henderson to him. He was low-keyed, enjoyed bantering with customers, liked being "Frank" of Frank's Place; he seemed comfortable with himself. He was maybe five-ten, not tall enough to challenge men to whom height mattered, but taller than most women. His light brown hair was just wiry enough to suggest that any moment it might snap back into little-boy curls. His eyes were blue, his skin sufficiently weathered to save him from the suggestion of effeteness (an important distinction in an area receiving a wave of gay emigrants from San Francisco). He wore the heavy gray fishing sweater favored by local fishing families. On Frank it looked not like the grubby garment of the docks, but rather like a sailing sweater. The city emigrants, gay and straight, found it a charming adaptation, and the old-time locals felt it signaled Frank's opting for them.

"Are you taking lunch early?" he asked.

"No, I'm sick."

"You don't look sick."

"In the eyes of PG&E, I have the flu."

"Oh. Does that mean the lights will go out all over town?"

"Alas. I don't quite have that power. All it signifies is that today's meters will be read tomorrow."

He leaned over the bar. "All those utility customers, standing by their meters, anxiously shifting from foot to foot, waiting for the big moment. Such disappointment."

"You, at least, can relax. I've already read your meter. And I meant to talk to you about it."

"Oh, no. Caught."

"No, no. You just ought to have your wiring checked. Most of the business tamperings are low —really gross underreadings. Sometimes I wonder if businessmen think PG&E hires only the retarded or the blind. I mean, when a grocery installs a new freezer and their consumption goes *down*, come on. . . ."

He laughed, a little-boy laugh that spread over his whole face.

"So what about me?" he said, the laughter absent from his voice.

"A little nervous, eh?"

When Frank didn't respond, I continued. "Relax. Your usage is really high. You're paying too much. You need your meter checked and probably your wiring. It's easy to do and it can save you fifty or sixty bucks a month."

"My bills aren't that high."

"Wait till you see this one. Yours was higher than usual last month, but the jump this month is outrageous. Something needs to be repaired. Either you have a pump that's not turning off, or a freezer on all the time, or your wiring in general is going. In any case, it's not going to fix itself."

"Okay, okay. When I get the chance, I'll think about it."

"In the meantime you will go on making charitable contributions to your local utility."

"It's not that much. I'll worry about it later. But now, how about a hot buttered rum for a sick lady?"

"At noon?"

"It'll do the trick at any hour."

"Okay, you're the bartender."

The rain poured down the outside of the windows behind the bar. In summer I had looked through them at the river. Frank had window boxes under them filled with pink and white impatiens. I had kidded him about his nice grandmotherly touch. But now the warmth of the room steamed the windows, turning them into foggy mirrors. As Frank heated the rum I eyed my impressionistic reflection. I could make out the brown hair hanging limp to my shoulders. I probably did look sick. When I had lived and worked in San Francisco, my hair had been short, cut in a crisp, competent account executive style. It had been one of my accoutrements that said: *This is a woman on her way up.* And when I moved to the river, the hairstyle was the first thing to go.

Still, I did have some make-up on, and I wasn't wearing khaki brown, so I must have looked better than I did at work.

"Your rum, my dear."

"Thanks. Aren't you going to join me?"

Frank hesitated. I suppose that question came up way too often for a bar owner.

"Sure. It'll be a slow day. Actually, real slow for me. I'm going to San Francisco late this afternoon."

"To see old friends?"

"Maybe. Two years takes its toll. I see fewer of the people I knew when I was living there. But it's still great to go back."

"Where did you live there?"

"In the Marina. I had a third-floor flat. A steal. I could see the sailboats coming in to dock every evening. And it was near Union Street and Fort Mason, so there was always good food, and theater, or concerts."

"That's what I miss up here. Even the movies. Sometimes I'd kill for a foreign film."

"It'll pass. You've only been here a year. By this time next spring, you'll only maim for it."

I leaned back against the wall behind the bar stool. I hadn't asked, but Frank refilled my glass. My 10 A.M. scrambled eggs were outclassed when it came to mopping up the alcohol. My head felt like the steamy windows. It was nice on a cold rainy day.

"Listen," Frank said. "Why don't you come with me? We can go to the theater in Japantown.

Or see what's going on at Fort Mason. If there's no live show there, we could at least have dinner."

"I don't know."

"Why not?"

"It'd sort of be cheating. This was my day to enjoy the solitude of my house."

Frank laughed. "That lasted a long time, didn't it? You made it to what, noon?"

"I guess so." I laughed, too. "That was one of the things I was going to change when I moved up here. I was going to be less dependent on other people. I was really going to discover the joy of being alone. Sort of a secular monk."

Frank put a hand on my shoulder. "There are worse things than enjoying people."

I laughed again. The rum gave the serious issues I had worried over rather a fanciful air. "I thought when I bought the house and moved in, that I would be living in the country, among country people. I thought it would be so different, that I would be forced to deal with solitude. But half the people I meet here are just like me—they've been out of the city less than two years—nouveau woodsy."

"It's true. In a sense, we're all spoiling the area for ourselves and everyone, particularly the old-time residents. If it gets any artsier, we may as well go back to the city."

"Perhaps." I didn't want the conversation to take this turn. It was depressing. "But, whatever, we'll go to the city this afternoon. Are you sure, Frank?" I said, smiling, "that none of your covey of new ladies will be demanding your attendance then?"

"Not me. I'm just an old bachelor bartender."

"You! The catch of the area. Is there one new lady you haven't been out with?"

He shrugged and favored me with that grin. "Surely," he said, "this is not jealousy."

"What? Not me. We're just friends, right?"

"Is that all?"

I laughed once more. I knew this line. I had heard Frank use it on every female customer who was still ambulatory. It charmed them all, just as it charmed me. "I loved our couple of dates last fall," I said, "but I really do like being friends even better. I would hate not to be told the tales of whom you're dating and whom you're not. And besides, you probably only take friends to the city in the afternoon."

"I . . ."

The telephone rang. Frank stepped around the corner and picked up the receiver.

The rain, which frequently let up during the day, was falling harder. Through the steamed windows, I could barely make out the river. I lowered myself off the stool, realizing suddenly that I was not quite steady. It was good that I hadn't sat long enough to have a third hot buttered rum. I wiped a circle of steam off the window behind the bar and stared through. The brown and opaque river bore no resemblance to the peaceful stream of summer on which tourists paddled Paul and Patsy Fernandez's canoes. Now it was rapids. It tossed branches, the length of a man, against the banks. If Frank's Place weren't on stilts, it would be flooded every spring. As it was, the floor had been covered with mud and silt during two or three of the worst floods.

"I'll be taking a lady friend with me," Frank was saying into the receiver.

I was not here last year. I bought the little house right after the rainy season. It was built high with a foundation on pinions sunk into the hillside. It was forty-some years old. I knew I had nothing to worry about, but, looking at the river smashing against its banks, I worried.

"I don't take orders." Suddenly Frank's voice was sharper. "But it isn't essential. I'll go alone. So, just forget it, will you?"

I walked back around the bar, climbed on the stool and waited, disappointed, angry, the rum magnifying my feelings. I knew how the liquor was affecting me, but that didn't make me less irritated.

It was only a minute before Frank hung up and was back leaning on the bar. His face showed no change, none of the anger that had been in his voice. I wondered if he were presenting me with his professional face. "Vejay," he said, "I'm sorry, really disappointed, but I'm going to have to take a raincheck"—he threw a wry look at the window —"on that trip to the city with you."

"Do you mean you're not going?" I tried to keep my voice neutral, my face as professional-looking as his. I suspected my performance wasn't up to his standards.

"No. It's just that the things I have to do there are going to require more of my attention than I thought."

"I'll bet." I didn't have to add, *She, whoever she is, wants all your attention.* Frank understood.

"No, Vejay. That's just being silly."

I stood up. "It's not being silly. I expected better

of you. I would expect that of any friend. I don't
like to be discarded when something better comes
along."

"It's not that. Believe me."

There was nothing more to say. I grabbed my
slicker, and stomped out the door, feeling at once
like Barbara Stanwyck in some old movie and like
any twelve-year-old. I knew that when the rum
wore off, any suggestion of Stanwyck would be
gone.

CHAPTER
2

My anger had propelled me down the steps before I stopped to put on my slicker. I was soaked. I stood there in the rain, pushing one and then the other thoroughly wet arm into the sleeves, then fiddled with the zipper. My truck was only twenty feet away. I could have run for it, without my slicker, and been drier.

When I looked up, zipper zipped, a battered black pickup was stopping in the lot. The horn blew a greeting and, before I could move, Chris Fortimiglio climbed out.

"Vejay. You off today?" Chris, tall and muscular, was one of those blond Italians. He was younger than I, maybe twenty-five, but already he was running the fishing business that had been in his family for three generations. The Fortimiglios were pillars of the old river families, never making much, but always surviving, always with some relative on the city council, or selling tickets for the St. Agnes pancake breakfast. There had been a period when fishing, particularly salmon fishing, provided a good income—when the Fortimiglios had added two bedrooms and a family room to their house—but now the whole area was overfished. The Russian trawlers came in close a couple of years. There had been an oil spill. The Fortimiglios were still surviving, but I knew that they closed off those new bedrooms in the winter, and the family room was used for storage.

"No. Listen, Chris, I'm sick. I'm supposed to be home. I should never have left the house. Don't tell anyone you saw me here, okay?"

"But why?" He moved closer, eyeing me diagnostically.

"I called in sick to work. If they suspected I wasn't really sick they could give me a bad time, even suspend me."

"Oh. Okay. But as long as you're here, why don't you come in and have something to drink?"

"No."

"Wow! You mad?"

"No. . . . Yes. I don't know. I'm just annoyed with Frank. I suppose it will pass."

"Did you have an argument?" It sounded so soap-opera-ish as he said it that I could almost see him recategorizing Frank's and my friendship. And I could see the entire Fortimiglio clan discussing it. And Sam Fortimiglio, Chris's uncle, worked for PG&E.

"No. It's nothing," I said. "But really, Chris, please don't mention to anyone that you saw me here today. Promise?"

"Sure."

"No one. Not even family."

"My family wouldn't . . ."

"No one."

He sighed. "Okay. It seems odd to me. But you city types do weird things. So, okay."

"Thanks, Chris." I squeezed his arm and headed to my truck. As I settled in the seat, I could see Chris start up the steps, stop, as if thinking, then turn and walk back to his pickup.

I hoped I didn't make Chris think badly of Frank. And I hoped I didn't make him ponder our whole conversation so much that he would find it impossible to resist discussing it.

I watched Chris pull out of the parking lot, but I didn't start my own engine. Instead I looked at the river rush over fallen branches, creating the beginnings of whirlpools. I could drive, but I knew I'd had enough to drink to make that legally questionable. All I needed now was to be stopped for drunk driving at 12:30, when I was supposed to be home sick. I had planned to take the day off, stay home, and luxuriate. My only stricture was to stay out of sight. I was certainly failing at that. So far my morning had been like "The Three Stooges Take a Sick Day."

My speculations were interrupted by the sound of an engine stopping. In the side parking lot, where Chris had been, I now saw the Chinese Laundry van, here to pick up Frank's napkins and tablecloths from the dinner trade. Frank's was mainly a bar, but he did have a few tables, and he served one entree per night—whatever Rosa Fortimiglio, Chris's mother, delivered. Customers never knew in advance whether they would be served ravioli, fettucini, or Salmon Rosa. But, whichever, it was always good, cheap, and filling.

The laundryman wouldn't know me, but I didn't want to be seen by another person, regardless. I eased my pickup around the far corner of the building and was pulling out onto the road before he had time to leave his truck.

It was still the noon hour. Traffic on the main bridge would be heavy. Pedestrians would be rushing to and from lunch. In the rain, the traffic

lights might go out at any time. It wouldn't be
wise for me to navigate through that. I didn't want
to be arrested, and I certainly didn't want to hit
anyone. So I turned west and drove away from
town, to the bridge a few miles down river. The
road was empty. Eucalyptus, fir trees, and redwoods crowded beside it, their wet branches hanging low, occasionally scraping the roof of the cab.
The headlights seemed to bounce off the rain; it
was like driving in a car wash.

I crossed the bridge and drove back along North
Bank Road. The river was maybe forty yards to
the right now. Between it and the road were a few
small shingle buildings. I had noticed them during
the summer. They were ill-painted, casually kept;
places that could be flooded with no great loss.
One was an abandoned café. It had been a soda
and coffee shop some years ago, but it had failed,
or the city person with dreams of running a country business had moved on to other projects. It
was in the same condition as the little houses.

North Bank Road started to become crowded as
I came into town. I turned left, bypassed the main
area of town and cut down the block before my
house, relieved to see no one out, and gratefully
pulled into the garage.

Back in the safety of my own house, I took a
long hot shower, then, prodded by guilt over my
wasted free day, I donned my slicker, grabbed two
empty half-gallon wine bottles, and trudged along
the muddy path that skirted the next two houses,
to the spring that provided the only palatable
drinking water. The stuff from the tap wouldn't
kill you, but it tasted too much like metal pipe. I
carried the full bottles to the house. Ten more

waited. I was beginning to get a headache. Picking up two more, I trudged back.

And, when the entire dozen were full, and I could be free from this joy of the country for another two weeks, I stoked the fire, took out a book on the architecture of Eureka that I had been planning to read for months, and promptly fell asleep.

It was four-thirty when I awoke, my mouth dry and cottony, my head aching, and the memory of my scene with Frank reminding me what an ass I had made of myself. So much for my luxuriant day.

But at least I felt sober. And I could make a decision. Frank might not have left for San Francisco yet. If he were still there, I could explain—apologize, sort of—though I didn't think I was entirely wrong. It just wasn't worth being unfriendly over. To make up, I could (openly, since it would be after five and after my working hours) show Frank how to read his meter and see that he was allowing himself to be overcharged. At a saving of fifty dollars a month, he would be well-recompensed for a few minutes of inconvenience.

After I had washed and dried my hair and spent a little time on my face and clothes, it was five-fifteen when I drove across the main bridge toward Frank's Place.

The side parking lot, where Chris had been, was full when I arrived. I had expected a couple of cars. Frank's opened officially at four-thirty. I pulled in, stopped, and, as I looked around, I realized that the cars were official. County sheriff cars. And a van.

I hurried up the steps to the bar. There was a

young officer at the door. No one, he told me, could go in.

"Is Frank okay?" I asked. "I'm a friend of his."

"Everyone's a friend of Frank's," he said. "But I can't let you in."

"What happened?"

"Frank's dead. Shot."

"What? But I was . . ."

The kid, the deputy, looked as shocked as I felt. He paid no attention to my abandoned sentence.

I stood, trying to decide what to do. It was hard, impossible, to imagine Frank dead—Frank, who was going to take me to a Japanese movie this evening. I needed to see Frank's body to believe he was dead. I waited, standing against the building wall.

The door opened. An older man stepped out. He nodded to the young officer, then looked at me.

"Who's she?" he said to the cop.

"She says she's a friend of Frank's."

"They're all friends of Frank's," he said, and it was apparent from his tone that the "they" he meant was female.

"What's your name?" he asked me.

"Vejay Haskell. Veronica Haskell."

"Haskell." His face lightened. He almost smiled. "Good. I want to talk to you. You're the one who was here at noon, the one who argued with Frank Goulet. I was going to send a squad car for you."

CHAPTER
3

Sheriff Wescott took me inside and sat me at one of the tables by the front window. I thought I needed to see Frank's body to convince me he was dead, but when I saw the oblong form covered by two tablecloths, it was enough. Plenty.

As I sat waiting for Sheriff Wescott, I thought how odd it was I was here, staring at Frank's corpse, when I had imagined I'd be sitting at the bar with Frank, apologizing for behaving like a jerk. I felt a tear roll down my cheek. It was irrational, I knew, but I hated to think that the last time Frank Goulet saw me I was slamming out of his bar. I took a breath and reminded myself that someone had come here afterward and shot Frank. There had been more important things on Frank's mind than my pique.

The section of Frank's Place where I sat held only eight tables. *Legal occupancy 44,* a sign said. It was cold by the window; Frank would have put the heat on an hour ago to warm the early customers. In another hour he would have turned it off. There would have been ample heat by now. I would have apologized; Frank would have shrugged it off and given me another hot buttered rum. I could use that now.

The sheriff sat in the chair opposite me. He was a neat, compact man about thirty-five with just the beginnings of age apparent on his face. His light, curly mustache was almost the same color as his skin. In ten years his hair would be dusted with gray and he would be described as "handsomely weathered." Now his features merely looked unsmoothed, as if he needed one more run through the factory before he could be marked finished.

"So you were here around noon, right?" he asked.

"Yes, but how did you know?"

"Tell me about that," he said, paying no heed to my question. But I didn't need his explanation. Coming out of the kitchen was Rosa Fortimiglio, Chris's mother. Chris had promised me silence. He meant it then. But Chris was no match for his mother, and gossip was as integral to the Fortimiglio clan as fishing or pasta. Now Rosa Fortimiglio was carrying two large jars of salmon-colored sauce toward the door. So the "audit-trail" of gossip was clear: Chris had told Rosa, and Rosa, making her evening delivery for Frank, had mentioned my stop to the sheriff.

As Rosa reached the door, she noticed me, stopped and, both arms full, nodded. There was no suggestion of embarrassment, no hint of a confidence broken. I knew that Rosa's mention of my being here at noon was not intended to incriminate me, but was rather a vote of confidence. It hadn't occurred to her that I might have been involved in Frank's death, so there was no less reason for her to mention me than to mention Chris.

"You were here at noon, Ms. Haskell," the sheriff said, his voice growing testy. "You were the last person to see Frank Goulet alive."

"No. Someone killed him. That person saw him alive."

"Someone." He let the word hang. "Tell me about your visit. How did you happen to be here on a Tuesday?"

I leaned forward on my elbows, ignoring the police officers who bustled around the other part of the room. "I came to talk to Frank about his electric meter. I'm a meter reader for PG&E."

"So you were on your rounds?"

"No. I had taken a sick day. I mean, I was sick. Nothing serious, but I was too sick to spend all day climbing up and down slippery stairways in the rain."

"You were too sick to go to work, but well enough to come here to a bar."

"There *is* a difference. You don't get pneumonia in a well-heated bar."

He sat back a little. "Okay, we'll skip any further medical diagnosis. You said you came here to talk about the electric meter. On your day off. Couldn't you have done that during your regular work hours? Wouldn't that have been more reasonable than dragging yourself out of your sick bed?"

"My employer," I said with exaggerated patience, "does not encourage us to make special trips to tell patrons they are paying too much. When a customer discovers he has been overcharged, he is not pleased to be informed; he is irate that he wasn't told sooner. We have to send someone out to make sure that the meter itself was not running too fast. We might have to check the appliances or the wiring. In any case, it costs PG&E money. And it's a hassle. So while we do inform customers, we don't go out of our way. You understand?"

"I understand." His tone mimicked mine. "But you *did* go out of your way."

Sheriff Wescott had been suspicious when he started questioning me. Everything I said seemed to make it worse. He was right—I had gone out of my way. "Well, Frank was a friend. And I was bored, and my house was cold, and I couldn't go anywhere else, because I was . . . sick." And this certainly didn't help.

"So you were here on a social call?"

"You could say that, but I did mention the meter."

"And how did Goulet react?"

"About the meter? He said fifty dollars one way or the other was no big thing."

"What else did you talk about?"

I tried to recall Frank and the bar at noon, when it had been so cozy and the rum had warmed me. "We talked about my being sick. He gave me a drink. We talked about San Francisco. Both of us lived in the city before coming here. Frank said he was going there late this afternoon, and he invited me to come."

"So that's why you're here now? You were expecting to meet him to go to the city?"

"Well, no. You see, he changed his mind."

"Then you talked to him after that, after you were here at noon?"

"No. He changed his mind while I was here."

"He invited you and, before you left, he told you not to come?" The exasperation in his voice was clear.

"We chatted about the city." I said deliberately.

"He invited me to come, maybe to see a foreign movie. Then the phone rang, he talked, and when he came back he said he couldn't take me."

"Why?"

"I don't know."

"Didn't you ask?"

It seemed illogical that I hadn't. "No. I had had two drinks. I was annoyed because I wanted to go with him. I figured Frank had talked to some girlfriend in the city and lined up something better than just an afternoon with a friend."

"Then why were you so angry?"

"Because I wanted to go to the city. Because I'd had two hot buttered rums. Because the d y, which would have been so nice, was turning out rotten. I didn't discuss it with Frank. I just told him he was being inconsiderate, and I left."

He glanced down at a notepad. " 'Slammed the door coming out' is how a witness described your departure."

"Dammit, that's the type of thing you do when you're angry. But Frank was alive when I left. Chris was here after me. I saw the laundry truck pull up. Talk to them."

The ambulance men were lifting Frank's body onto a stretcher. The cloth covering his face caught on the rail of the bar. As they lifted him, it pulled back. His face was already gray. I could see the black of the gunpowder and the maroon of the dried blood on his forehead. I remembered Frank standing behind the steamy bar, his hand on my shoulder telling me that hot buttered rum was just the thing for a "sick lady." I cried.

When they carried Frank's body out, I looked back at the sheriff. I expected him to go on ques-

tioning me. It was apparent that he didn't believe
me. But he only demanded an account of my time
(not something that made me any less suspect,
since I so carefully kept out of sight all day). And
he told me not to leave the area.

I must have still looked weepy as I headed for
the door because Rosa Fortimiglio, coming back
in, stopped, put an arm around my shoulder and
informed me that I was coming to her house for
dinner. "I got all this fettucini," she said, nodding
toward the kitchen, "that's not going to be eaten
here."

The Fortimiglio house was at the west end of
town, nearer to the inlet and the fishing docks. In
the summer, the entire extended family sat on the
long porch. But now, in winter, they congregated
in the oddly shaped living room that had resulted
from the latest remodeling plan. The room was
oblong, with a couple of unexplained nooks and
an indentation around the stairs to the family
room. At one end, by the kitchen, a brick fireplace
occupied most of the wall. It provided more cheer
than heat. Tonight an electric heater buzzed at the
other end.

It was only seven o'clock. Rosa and I had been
out of Frank's Place less than half an hour.
Frank's body had been discovered only at four-
thirty when Rosa brought the fettucini, but the
word had spread and people had come here as if
beckoned by a church bell. Chris and his brothers-
in-law were in the kitchen, beers in hand, cadging
tastes of fettucini. Skip Bollo stood talking to the
Fortimiglio daughters while their children scam-
pered from them to their grandfather, in the

kitchen. Chris's father, Carlo, sat near the fire, his left leg propped up on the ottoman. He had injured it five years ago. No longer steady enough to stand all day on a fishing boat, he now drove his old truck around town, checking and bolstering the stilts under low-lying houses, carting summer people's possessions to higher ground, or taking debris to the dump. A quiet man in any season, he seemed to save his few words for his family and now, after a long day of pre-flood work, even responding to his grandchildren seemed an effort.

Rosa bustled to and from the kitchen, carrying plates to the card table, adjusting silver, piling up paper napkins. No one but Madge Oombs helped; we all knew the rules.

I walked over to Paul and Patsy Fernandez. They stood by the steamed windows that looked out onto the porch. With their long, straight black hair and bright, blue eyes they resembled a set of matching dolls. They looked more like brother and sister than the married couple they were. In jeans, workshirts, and cowboy boots, they were even dressed alike.

"It's hard to believe Frank is dead," Patsy said. "Killed. Shot. It's so . . . gangland."

"Like something you'd find in Oakland or San Francisco," Paul said.

"Frank came from San Francisco," I said.

"Yes," Paul agreed, "but that was two years ago." Involuntarily we both glanced toward Patsy. Normally pale, tonight her skin was almost as gray as Frank's. She clutched a glass of red wine. Patsy had liked Frank. In fact, when she and Paul had taken over the canoe rental here last year, there had been speculation about her and Frank. It had died quickly when Frank was seen with several attractive summer people.

Patsy looked like she would have been better off with a quiet drink at home this evening, but I suspected neither Paul nor Patsy had seriously considered declining a free meal. They could be generous and they could spend money (those cowboy boots weren't cheap) but there was something about them—a stain of the sixties—that would always make a free meal irresistible.

"Frank had left the city behind," Paul said. "This was his place now."

"If you think that," I said, "then it would follow that someone here shot him."

"No, I don't . . ."

"Of course not," I said quickly. "Did the sheriff question you?"

"He tried," Paul said defiantly. Another vestige of the sixties. Beside him, Patsy shrank back and stiffened.

"We couldn't tell them much," Paul continued. "We were in Santa Rosa all day getting supplies. As soon as the river floods, the county will commandeer our canoes. And they'll bring them back banged up. They're always pleased to have them for their rescues, but no one's ever around when they need to be repaired."

Patsy nodded absently.

"And our county government doesn't feel any responsibility to pay. They shifted us from one department to another last year when we asked," Paul said.

"How well did you know Frank?"

He stopped, startled. I had heard the monologue of complaint before and knew it was nowhere near half done. Still, it amazed me how quickly he had forgotten Frank.

Regrouping, he said, "Frank was always friendly; he was helpful, if it didn't put him out. You know what I mean?"

I nodded.

"We saw him at the bar mostly."

"Did you know him in San Francisco?" I asked.

"No. No way. Frank wouldn't have been living like we were, not in the Haight, not eating off food stamps, not going door to door collecting for whatever cause was paying solicitors. Frank must have lived pretty high there. After all, he could afford to buy a restaurant here."

I almost commented that they had afforded the lease on the boat rental concession, but that would have directed Paul back to his finances, and I didn't have the patience to listen to that, much less sympathize with it.

Fortunately, the fettucini was on the card table and people were lining up. Rosa Fortimiglio ladled the noodles and Carlo, her husband, the clam sauce.

"Poor Frank," Rosa said, as she piled more noodles on my plate than I had any hope of consuming. "This was one of his favorites. He was always pleased on the days I brought him fettucini. But the calamari, that was the only thing he ever asked for."

I nodded. Rosa's delivery service had been a good arrangement for both Frank and Rosa. For Frank, it kept customers from leaving to find dinner, and then perhaps not returning. With Rosa's dinners, many of us spent all evening at Frank's.

And for the Fortimiglios, it provided some steady income to offset the capriciousness of fishing.

I sat down next to Madge Oombs and Ned Jacobs, the ranger at the state park near town. Ned was dark, wiry, and reminded me of one of the chipmunks it was his job to protect. He was about my age, a bit over thirty. His family had had a summer place here when he was a child, and though his winters had been spent in Oakland, it was the Russian River that had stamped him. He had studied not law, as his family had intended, but forestry, then taken the necessary jobs in less desirable areas until he had the seniority to get back here. Now he was home.

"How could something like this happen?" he was saying. "Here. To Frank. It must be some connection from when he lived in San Francisco. Or maybe one of the new people." Ned always referred to the homosexuals and other emigrants from San Francisco, who had "discovered" the Russian River a year or two ago and were on the way to making it their own, as the "new people." He wanted to make it clear that he didn't care about their habits, he cared that they were disrupting his town. "Maybe they tried to get Frank to be a middleman in a drug deal, and Frank refused, and then they killed him. That would make sense, wouldn't it?"

"I suppose it would, as well as anything else," I said. "There are enough drugs in the area. And Frank was shot."

"But it was with his own gun." Rosa Fortimiglio pulled up a wooden chair and sat across from Ned. I realized, as she spoke, that I had been too startled to ask Sheriff Wescott anything about

Frank's death, but Rosa wouldn't have made that mistake. "It was with his own gun," she continued, "the one he kept in the bar. You remember last summer, when he had to threaten two big drunks with it?"

We all nodded.

"Outsiders," Ned added.

"Shot him," Rosa said. "Wiped the fingerprints off the gun and left it on the bar. Cool as can be."

"Outsiders," Ned said.

Madge Oombs, who had been sitting quietly, shook her head. "How would an outsider get there? Would they drive right up the street? The sheriff checked on that. They asked the old people who live on the hill across from Frank's Place. There are three of them, you know. They don't miss a thing. They sit by the window, watching the road, all day. They didn't see any strangers drive up there. They didn't notice anyone come after Chris. Isn't that right, Rosa?"

"Not a soul, so they said." It was obvious that the two friends had carried on an in-depth discussion in the kitchen while Rosa heated the fettucini.

"So how did they get there, Ned?" Madge demanded.

"Parked and walked?" he suggested. But, even as he said it, we all knew it was wrong.

"Ned," Madge said, "there'd be no reason for an outsider to park half a mile away and trudge through the rain, on a road that has no sidewalk—only mud at either edge. They couldn't know about the old folks staring out the window. And besides, the lawns are so flooded now that any pedestrian would have to walk in the middle of the street, and you don't think those old folks would miss that, do you?"

"Well, no." Ned's lips were pursed. He hated to have the outsiders cleared so quickly. "Then how did the murderer get there if he didn't drive and he didn't walk?"

We all knew, but we waited for Madge to say it. "The river. Someone came down the river, past the empty houses that the summer people use. They came up to the hidden dock under the bar and up through the trap door."

We all knew what that meant, but again we waited for it to be put into words. Rosa said it. "It's possible that a stranger might know the trap door existed, he might have heard about liquor being cooled in the water below during Prohibition. But no stranger would be able to find a small boat and get it downriver with the water like it is today, find the inlet into Frank's, do his deed, and get the boat back. No outsider."

CHAPTER
4

Not surprisingly, I didn't sleep well that night. Rain hit the windows in gusts; eucalyptus branches slapped against the house. I should have had the trees trimmed last fall, as the neighbors had suggested. Now the ground was soaked and wouldn't support such tall trees. They would crash into the house. I wouldn't have to worry about being implicated in Frank Goulet's murder; I would be dead.

When the sky finally lightened to the dim gray of dawn, I was relieved. Even the iciness of the house was preferable to staying in bed. By six-thirty I was up, dressed, and on my way to Thompson's to get my paper.

Since I was early, I went to the café for breakfast. It was nearly empty. On clear mornings it was filled with laborers from the sewer project. They had been working on that sewer so long that they were regulars there. They jammed into the booths, shouting, laughing, calling for more coffee, playing the juke box. Anyone else lucky enough to get a seat on one of those mornings found it impossible to talk or read. So most people avoided the café before eight. Now, in the rainy season, with the sewer work suspended, the café was empty and quiet. I was glad to be able to sit alone in a back booth and read the paper.

The newspaper coverage of Frank's murder filled two columns on the front page and several on page six, but it told me nothing new. And, thank God, it didn't mention names. So, although everyone in town would know I was at Frank's Place yesterday, it was still possible that my boss might not.

Taking no chances on that, I got to the Henderson substation early and by ten after eight I had put in a sick card for the previous day, picked up the day's route book, and signed out the most reliable truck in the yard. I was out of the office before most people had come in.

The rain was heavier than it had been the day before. The river was higher and the water was thick with debris.

It was good to have a truck that wouldn't break down, one with new tires and an engine that could pull it out of the mud. I would be "dragging the truck" today—walking house to house for a couple hundred yards, then coming back to move the truck along so I would have it for parts of the route where there were long driveways and distances between houses.

The route was assigned. The pages of the route book were in order, one page per customer, up one side of the street and down the other. But few readers followed that plan. There were always ways the route could be altered to suit one's personal idiosyncracies. Some readers started at the west end of their routes and worked east each day, moving away from the ocean, as if every hundred yards would diminish the cold dampness of the Pacific. Some read commercial accounts first, residences last. Some did the flatlands in the morning in hopes that by afternoon, when they had to climb those endless wooden stairs, the rain would have stopped. I did the stairs first, before I was fully awake and aware of my aching thighs, and saved the flats till later, when just the thought of another step was debilitating.

This route was divided into two sections. The first part, including South Bank Road and Frank's Place, I had done Monday. The remainder of the route was set up to start with a group of cottages on the ocean side of town. The Fortimiglios' was among them. If I did the hillside first, I could work down to their meter well before noon.

I parked the truck halfway up the hill and checked through the route book. Each page had spaces to list the customer's usage for twenty-four months, so I could see how much electricity they used this time last year. If their present usage was dramatically higher, like Frank's, it raised questions. If it was considerably lower, the questions became suspicions. Before starting out, I glanced through the upcoming twenty or so pages for houses on this block, checking the comments section on each page. There were a number of places noted "dog OK," a few merely "dog," and only one "dog/w" (watch out). Although the location of the meter was mentioned on each page, I found it faster to follow the service drop from the main line to the weatherhead above the actual meter.

I walked quickly on the streets and carefully down unpaved, muddy driveways to meters on the sides of houses. The houses were stuck like magnets on the hillside. "OK dogs" came out for a sniff of me, and just "dog" dogs looked warily before backing off. In the newer houses, the meters were around back, over ground that had been cleared out and not reseeded, and which was now a pool of mud. Older ramshackle places had their weatherheads above innocent-looking patches of weeds that too often turned out to be abandoned cesspools. The rotted wood of the cesspools was never equal to the weight of the unsuspecting reader. I was thankful when one had been abandoned long enough to be dry.

A number of places—summerhouses—were empty, their service turned off. The route went fast. I was almost to the end of the hillside section when I came to the Kellys' house. There was an "R" in the Changes column on their pages: last month the reader had found their meter tampered with. Most likely, the Kellys had broken the seal, pulled the meter out, and turned it over so it would run backwards. Every kilowatt hour they used would have saved them money. The reader had turned the meter right side up, resealed it, and stuck a warning sticker on it. Until recently, it had been rare for the warning to be followed by any real penalty, and the likelihood of a repeat was great. And indeed, the Kelly meter was upside down again.

I laughed. The Kellys only needed to call the office to find what day I would be here. If they had controlled their greed and turned it back after a few days, even a week, I might not have noticed the difference in usage from last year. But greed is greed. Or sloth is sloth. Whichever, the Kellys had neglected to turn it back over. I marked the Changes column and left the meter. A fraud investigator would be out the next day.

I dragged the truck up and did two accounts at

the top of a long steep driveway, then I parked and walked for the next six houses. Beyond there, the street was washed out. The hillside beneath one of the new houses had given way. The house, a wooden chalet with the inevitable deck hanging off it, jutted out over the bare, concave hillside. The house would survive—it was on deep pillars, sunk into the rockiness of the hillside—but the street, completely covered in dirt, wouldn't be shoveled out till summer.

Irritated, I turned back. I would have to drive around, and that would use up all the time I had saved—time I had planned to spend at the Fortimiglios'.

It was twelve-fifteen when I got to their house. Rosa was at the door before I reached the meter.

"Come in, Vejay. Dry off. We're just thinking of lunch. It's lucky you got here now."

Sheepishly, I thanked her for the invitation. It was hardly luck.

Carlo sat in the kitchen, while Rosa stirred something on the stove that smelled of spiced tomato. From the living room I could hear the television and the low rumble of voices.

"Take your boots off and let them dry by the stove," Rosa said.

As I did that, Carlo poured three glasses of red wine. I sat and, disregarding the headache I still had from the rum and wine yesterday, I took a sip.

"It's terrible about poor Frank," Rosa said, as if returning to an interrupted thought. "The person who killed him couldn't have been anyone local, not from town. The way Frank was shot, in the forehead, someone had to be looking right at him. You wouldn't do that to a person you know."

"You might," I said, "if you were angry enough to kill him."

"Well, perhaps," Rosa said without conviction. "But who would feel that way about Frank? He didn't have any enemies here, not even any real business competition."

"Drugs," Carlo said.

Rosa was silent, and I turned to him in surprise —not so much at what he said, but at the fact that he had spoken at all. I doubted whether I had ever heard Carlo offer an unsolicited comment. Frank's death must have affected him deeply.

"You were close to Frank, weren't you?" I said to him.

He nodded.

"Frank was always over here at first," Rosa said. "You know he and Chris were friends. That's how Frank came up here. Chris and Frank were in the Navy together. Chris can tell you about that. Chris!" she called without missing a beat. "Chris, Vejay's here."

I heard the television go silent. Chris and a teenage boy I recognized as one of the Fortimiglio grandchildren walked into the kitchen. They both wore jeans and woollen shirts. It was the slack season for fishing, so Chris was home. It took only one look at the boy's red, running nose to see why he wasn't in school.

"Chris, I was telling Vejay how you were in the Navy with Frank," Rosa said.

"That's right." Chris directed his reply to me. "I was going to make a career of it. I went in right after high school. It was okay, the Navy, for that time. But it wasn't like here, where it's our boat, our fish, our family business."

Chris took a beer from the refrigerator. "But Frank, it was different for him. He wasn't like anyone else on the ship." He laughed. His parents looked at him, slightly shocked, as if it were too soon to laugh about Frank. "The thing was that Frank really hated being on ship. I guess he didn't think of that part when he signed up."

"It would seem to be a major oversight," I said.

" 'Join the Navy and see the world!' Frank loved the ports. He was always the first off and the last back on ship. And he bought more stuff than any five guys. Not the normal junk either. He knew what he was getting. He'd study up while we were at sea. He really hated being taken. That's how he got into studying up, see?"

I waited for Chris to continue.

"One time," Chris said, "I think it was in Taipei, Frank bought a jade figurine. He paid a lot for it, and when he got back on ship he was showing it around and one of the officers had a look. He knew right off that Frank had been had. It was no rare yellow jade, like Frank thought. It was yellow glass! We all had a big laugh over that. Everyone but Frank. He was furious. If the ship hadn't been pulling out, he would have hunted down the guy who sold it to him."

"But instead he started reading up on jade?" I prompted.

"Right. He bought a lot of jade. And later, net-sukes, you know, those tiny Japanese carvings, the ones with lots of little animals all on top of each other? They're only a couple inches tall."

I nodded. I'd seen netsukes at the Asian Art Museum.

"Anyway," Chris continued, "Frank hated every minute he was on ship. I think he was actually seasick a few times. Of course, he wouldn't admit it—the guys would have ribbed him to death. He got enough flack as it was. He was really a step above most of us. He was older; he'd been to college. He wasn't just interested in the body count in every port, if you know what I mean." Chris looked sheepishly away from Rosa.

"Your mother said Frank came up here because of you."

Chris smiled. "Well, I wouldn't put it that way. That makes it sound a little odd between us. No. After Frank got out of the Navy, I didn't see him much. I shipped out again. Then after my discharge I'd go down to San Francisco when the fishing was slow."

"What was Frank doing in San Francisco?"

"Drinking, when he was with me." Chris laughed. "But you mean, for work? Nothing regular. He got jobs, stayed with them till he had enough money, then quit and travelled. Then he'd come back and find another job."

"Do you think he was smuggling?" I asked in a fit of inspiration.

Chris considered a moment. "I doubt it, Vejay. He never had much money. When he came back from a trip, he usually had to sell some of his figurines to get by until he found work. And I picked him up at the airport once. He hadn't shaved; his jeans were ripped; his shirt was a mess. I don't think a smuggler would dress like that."

"Not more than once," I said, laughing.

"Time to eat." Rosa put plates of spaghetti before us, on the kitchen table.

The teenage Fortimiglio sneezed, dug a handkerchief from his pocket, blew his nose, and then enthusiastically attacked his spaghetti. Aside from his sneezing, he seemed to be even quieter than his grandfather.

Rosa touched Chris's arm. "Tell Vejay about the canoe trip," she said.

Chris laughed again. This time no one looked surprised. "Frank decided, for old times' sake, we would take a boat trip. We'd paddle a canoe from the inlet up to town. It was a good time of the year for that. The river was calm, the water was low. So I said, fine. I got a canoe from a friend of Pop's by the inlet. . . ."

"I didn't know they had canoes there," I said.

"They're not for rental. This guy just loaned it to us, right, Pop?"

Carlo nodded as he twirled the spaghetti against his spoon.

"So, Frank and I paddled up river. This time he *was* sick. I mean, we had to stop for him to throw up. But he insisted on paddling all the way to the far side of town. He said he promised himself he could do it, and he didn't want to welsh on himself."

"But he didn't take the canoe back, did he, Chris?" Rosa laughed.

"No. He offered, sort of. But he was real glad when I said I could do it alone."

"Why *did* Frank decide to move here?" The spaghetti slipped off my fork. I considered cutting it, but decided against it. I started to wind again.

Chris looked momentarily confused. "Oh, you

did ask that, didn't you? I hadn't seen him for a
couple months. He just called and said he was
tired of the city and wanted to get away. So—you
know Mama—she told me to invite him up. He
stayed for a week and he loved it."

For Chris there was no need to explain Frank's
reaction. Loving the Russian River was natural.

"I guess Frank had heard me talk about the
river so much when we were on ship—I was pretty
homesick then—that he felt like he knew it. I must
have talked about the town and everybody here
twenty hours a day. Later, even now, I talk about
it a lot. I'd told Frank so much that when he first
came here he recognized people right off. He never
had to ask where anything was."

"How did he afford the Place?"

"He sold all his figurines."

"They must have been worth quite a bit."

"That's what the sheriff said. Frank told me he
got taken once selling a netsuke, so when he sold
the lot he knew what to ask."

"The sheriff was here?"

Chris stuffed a forkful of spaghetti into his
mouth, looking toward his mother as he chewed.
It was apparent he was passing the conversation to
her.

Rosa put down her fork slowly. "The sheriff—
Sheriff Wescott—came by this morning, asking
about Frank. There wasn't much we could tell
him."

"What did he say?"

Rosa hesitated. She looked embarrassed. I had
never seen Rosa have a second thought about discussing a conversation, particularly one so obviously in the public domain.

"Did he tell you something about Frank?" I asked.

"No, no. Nothing we all don't know. He asked about Frank, and then, Vejay, he asked about you. You and Frank. I told him there was no reason for him to suspect anything there, that he was wasting his time."

"Is that all he said? About me, I mean."

"Well, no." Rosa took an unusually long sip of her wine. She put the glass down slowly. "He asked how well we knew you, and we told him. We told him you were a friend, a good friend, that he'd do better to believe you and not spend his time foolishly asking questions about you when he should be looking for Frank's killer." Rosa smiled. "He didn't like being told that."

"Thanks," I said.

"No need for that," she said. "I told him if you said you were sick, then you were sick."

"Thanks," I repeated without much enthusiasm. I did appreciate Rosa's faith in me. But the sheriff wouldn't. He knew I hadn't been sick. Now he would think Rosa had no discrimination when it came to me. How many people, I wondered, was he questioning about me? Was I the focus of the investigation?

"Drugs," Carlo said.

"What?" I said, shaking off my speculations.

"Carlo reminded the sheriff about the drugs," Rosa added quickly, with a clear relief at the change of subject.

"All the drugs that go through here, there's bound to be violence," Carlo said. "There's a lot of money in marijuana."

Carlo sat in his wool fisherman's sweater, the

wine glass held momentarily before his craggy Italian face. I was always surprised when he spoke —not only because he was usually so quiet, but also because he had no trace of an accent. Though he was in his late fifties, his hair was only partly gray, his face weathered from those years fishing at sea. He was a small man, but his arms and shoulders were well-muscled, perhaps in compensation for his injured leg.

"They grow marijuana up north. They drive it through here to San Francisco. Bound to be crime. Frank must have got caught in it. Maybe he had connections in San Francisco. I told the sheriff that." Carlo put down the wine glass, signaling the end of his statement. He had said more in these few minutes than I had heard him say in the entire year I had lived here. Usually he sat comfortably in the background, watching Rosa make everyone at home, listening to Chris and his brothers-in-law talk about the fish, watching his daughters and their children.

Now he pushed himself up, nodded, and headed for the door.

As the door shut after him, Rosa said to me, "He's going to dig a trench behind the Millers' house on the High Road. Last year the water caused a lot of damage there. It's busy for him this time of year. People need a lot done right before the flood comes." She stacked our plates and carried them to the sink. "It's good for him to have these jobs," she added, with her back still toward me. "It was hard, so hard for him, after he got hurt. He couldn't keep his balance on the boat. He couldn't fish anymore. He tried. . . . But this is good."

I wished I could say something comforting to Rosa, like she did for me yesterday, but what? Still, there was a diversion I could offer. I said, "Yesterday morning, I drove to the freeway to get my newspaper. And, in the restaurant there, guess who I saw together?"

Rosa turned, thinking, probing her collection of facts and possibilities, then giving up. "Who?"

"Madge Oombs and Skip Bollo."

"What?" Chris laughed.

"Now, Chris," Rosa said. She and Madge had been friends since grammar school.

"But, Mama, Madge and Skip!"

"I didn't say it was romantic," I said.

"I shouldn't think!" Chris was still laughing.

"Now you know what I know," I said, as I stood up to leave.

Both Rosa and Chris urged me to stay, but I had my route to finish. I needed to be alone to think through Frank's possible drug involvement, Frank's murder, and how suspect I appeared to the sheriff.

Rosa and Chris, I would leave with more pleasant thoughts—wonderfully intriguing speculations —that would last the rest of the afternoon. And I was certain I assured Madge a dinner invitation.

Even the Fortimiglios suspected Frank's death had been drug-related. I hadn't considered the question. But once it had been raised, the likelihood was so great I was surprised I hadn't thought of it myself. Millions of dollars worth of marijuana passed through here every year, coming from the wild country to the north, heading for the cities down south. And Frank was in an ideal position to be a middleman. It was definitely something to think about.

I pulled the truck into the parking lot behind the Henderson PG&E substation.

The substation was a three-room stucco storefront that accommodated customers in the front, the manager's office in the middle, and the storeroom that doubled as a meter readers' area at the rear. There we congregated in wet and cramped fellowship amidst tan metal cases of miscellaneous metal supplies, a scarred wooden table, a coat rack, a pegboard for the route keys, the Lazy Susan holding the route books, and the dufflebaglike, tan San Francisco bag that awaited the completed books. Each night the books in the San Francisco bag were rushed, via Santa Rosa, to the computer in San Francisco.

We readers rarely had reason to be in the customers' area. We ventured forward to Mr. Bobbs's

office (a tiny windowless cubicle that was one of
his few management perks) only to present him
pages from the route books on which tampering
had been recorded. He never came into our room.

So it was a shock to find him standing between
the cable wires and the San Francisco bag when I
arrived. His sallow face was orange with outrage;
his hand clasped hard over the tan canvas bag.

"We've had the sheriff here," he said before I
could put down the route book. "A Sheriff Wescott. He was asking about you."

"Me?" Why was the sheriff asking about me?
Why wasn't he checking on Frank's activities?

"He wanted to know about your duties as a
meter reader."

That seemed stranger yet.

"Your duties to your accounts."

"Yes?"

"He said, Miss Haskell, that you went to Goulet's bar for the purpose of reporting that his reading was too high. The sheriff asked if that was
within the scope of your duties."

I waited, startled that the sheriff questioned my
statements. What I had told him was true.

"I explained to the sheriff that, as you were
sick, you had no duties." Mr. Bobbs stared
straight at me, a move as abnormal for him as
entering the supply room. His face was still an
unnatural orange, his neck muscles so tight he was
barely breathing.

"What I am asking you, Miss Haskell, is how
do you explain that?"

I didn't know exactly what he was asking. Did
he want an explanation of Frank's overread, my
reporting it, or the sheriff's visit? I suspected it

was the last. Mr. Bobbs took his position as manager very seriously. As he was quick to say, he had been in power (electricity) for twenty years. It was a standing joke among the readers that he dressed in a tan suit to match the San Francisco bag. One day, in a flurry, he would be mistaken for it, rushed to the city, and fed into the computer.

But even if he were asking why I had decided to go to Frank's Place, I couldn't fully explain, not to myself, and certainly not to him. Predominantly, it was in response to a feeling that I got from Frank for the past few weeks. Frank had seemed uneasy with me, distant. I couldn't think of a reason. I was uncomfortable, then annoyed, and confused. The issue had to be discussed; I'd avoided it as long as . . . I guess now I'd avoided it forever.

To Mr. Bobbs I said, "Since I was there I decided to mention the overread. It was considerable. His usage had been regular up to the last month or so."

"Regular for twenty years."

It was like Mr. Bobbs to be able to recall the figures of an individual account.

"There's been a bar at that account since the twenties," he said. "Never problems, our problems. Disputes with the law during Prohibition, they say, but no usage problems."

I waited, but he said nothing more. He stood looking somewhere beyond my left shoulder, but he made no move to return to his office.

Anxious to keep the topic impersonal, I said, "Speaking of problems, there was another tampering at the Kellys' on the High Road."

"Have you warned the account?" Mr. Bobbs always referred to customers as accounts, as if peo-

ple were created merely to be instruments for the
consumption of electricity.

"I stuck a warning on the meter last month.
And yesterday the meter was running backwards
again." I put the route book on the table and
flipped to the Kelly page. Mr. Bobbs glanced down
at the "R" in the Changes column.

"Umm. Tampering last month *and* this month.
I'll get the investigator from Santa Rosa. Tomorrow, first thing."

"There's a slide on that road from last year. It'll
be worse by tomorrow." I unzipped my slicker.

Mr. Bobbs continued to stare at the offending
page. "Two months straight, with a warning . . ." He removed the page, closed the book
with a snap, and placed it carefully in the San
Francisco bag.

I was just reaching in my pocket for the keys
that accompanied the route when he said, "Two
days off."

"What?"

"You will be suspended for two days."

"But why?"

"Abuse of sick leave."

"I don't need an excuse for one sick day."

His hand tightened on the San Francisco bag.
"You weren't sick, Miss Haskell. The sheriff told
me you were at Goulet's bar, drinking. At noon.
Two drinks." His voice was squeaky, his breath
caught in those viselike neck muscles. "You were,
Miss Haskell, tampering with the sick leave pol-
icy."

He held up a page from the personnel manual.
"Sick leave may be requested by an employee in

cases of personal illness. Up to three days leave *may* be granted without medical verification."

"I turned in a sick card this—"

He continued. "If there is question as to the appropriateness of the request, medical verification is necessary. There *is* question. Clearly, you do not have medical verification of your 'illness.' " He put down the page. "Two days off."

I stared, infuriated, then turned and stalked out, not bothering to avoid slamming the door. It wasn't until I had crossed the parking lot and climbed into my own pickup that I realized I still had the route keys in my pocket. I wasn't about to return them.

I drove out of the lot, barely aware of the road. Three days off! The more I thought of it the angrier I became. Technically, Mr. Bobbs was within his rights. I hadn't been really sick. I might have been, for all he knew. I might have had a sore throat, or a touch of the flu, but I didn't. Still, that day I couldn't have faced another eight hours tramping up those staircases in the rain. By March "illness" was rampant among meter readers, and the unspoken rule was that if you had accrued sick time, it was yours to use, as long as you kept a low profile. And two days suspension was certainly extreme punishment.

But furious as I was, it was unsatisfying to focus it on Mr. Bobbs. I still pictured him clutching the San Francisco bag. The scene clearly had upset him as much as it had me; he had been tense to the point of breathlessness. It was another standing joke among the readers that at 5 P.M. Mr. Bobbs dropped headfirst into the San Francisco bag and pulled the tie closed over his feet. The Henderson substation was his life. And my "sick day" had made a mockery of it.

But Sheriff Wescott was another matter. I had assumed what I'd told him was in confidence, not something to be blabbed all over town. Certainly not information to be tattled to my employer. What was he doing asking about me, anyway? Didn't he have a murderer to catch?

I turned left onto North Bank Road. It wasn't raining now, but the rain had been so heavy so long that the streets were glazed with mud and leaves. As I braked at the light, my tires slipped on the road.

Three blocks beyond, I pulled into my driveway, turned off the engine, and pushed the electric garage door opener before I realized I was too furious to sit in an empty house.

I closed the garage door and shifted the truck into reverse, ready to drive to Frank's Place to lean on the bar and bitch. But I couldn't do that anymore. Ever again.

I was going to miss Frank more than I'd realized.

Saddened, but no less angry, I backed out and headed for Guerneville, where the sheriff had his office.

CHAPTER

6

I drove along North Bank Road, past the new boutique-y shops and summer businesses that had sprung up in the last couple of years, past specialty florists and western wear shops, fast-food restaurants, and rental agencies. In a few days they would be under water. I muttered at people backing out from the few open establishments. I held the wheel hard against the slippery road. I was driving too fast and I knew it, but I didn't slow down.

The closer I got to Guerneville, the angrier I became. The sheriff's comments at the Henderson substation had caused Mr. Bobbs a great deal of anguish and would cost me three days' wages.

I pulled up in front of the modern aluminum structure that houses the Sheriff's Department and headed inside.

"I need to see Sheriff Wescott," I said to the officer at the desk.

"Your name?"

"Veronica Haskell."

"Is he expecting you?"

"No. But I need to see him now."

"He's in a conference—"

"I'll wait."

There was quite a controversy when this building was being constructed. The glass and aluminum structure did not fit in with the natural woodsiness of Guerneville. Many residents, notably the more recent immigrants drawn to the area by its charm, found the starkness of the building an affront. The best they could say was that it was not situated downtown. It was almost at the city limits, and hardly visible to those who didn't have business here. Ned Jacobs, the park ranger, had told me about it. He said it had ruined the town, that the architect was an outsider, which explained the "plastic box" structure. Being on the edge of town hadn't excused it in his mind.

I looked out through the rain-splattered windows at the puddles that covered nearly half of the side parking lot, and beyond to the eucalyptus.

"Miss Haskell?"

Sheriff Wescott stood behind the counter. Somehow, he seemed out of place here, away from the darkened atmosphere of the bar at Frank's. Under the fluorescent lights, it was apparent that his hair was not as light as I had thought, but a medium brown. His face still looked unfinished, though. And from his mustache a few extra-curly hairs poked out in odd directions.

"Right this way, into the inner recesses," he said, smiling a surprisingly easy smile as he pulled open the half-door in the counter. I followed him down a plexiglass corridor to an eight-by-ten office on the side of the aisle away from the windows. Back here the light blue plexiglass walls didn't reach the ceiling and the buzzing of typewriters, ringing of phones, and medley of conversations beyond gave me the feeling of entering a crowded maze rather than a private office.

Wescott plucked a newspaper from the light

blue visitor's chair, pulled the chair an inch closer to his desk, and motioned me to it. "Coffee?"

"No thanks," I said, sitting. The office seemed even smaller than eight-by-ten now. A blue file cabinet stuck out from one wall behind Wescott. A blue bookcase filled with official-looking volumes and stacks of papers stood alongside the desk, and several cardboard boxes were piled at the other side. He had to step over one of them to get to his chair.

He settled back. "You made the right decision about the coffee. It's from a machine and by the end of the day it tastes like the grease from the cogs." He smiled again and shifted a pile of papers to the side of his desk.

"This isn't a social call," I said.

"Oh?"

"I've been suspended from my job."

"You have?" He sounded truly surprised and concerned.

"My boss has suspended me for two days, for abusing sick leave."

He waited, his expression unchanged.

"He said you told him I was at Frank's Place on my sick day, drinking. Specifically, having two drinks."

Wescott leaned forward. "Oh, I'm sorry." He sounded sorry and surprised.

I didn't expect that.

"I did tell him you were there, Miss Haskell," he said. "You see, in a murder investigation we have to follow every lead even if it causes witnesses some difficulty. We don't deliberately, um, inconvenience people, but we do have to do everything we can to find the murderer. It's not always a fair process. Innocent people get their toes stepped on. We work on the theory of the greater good. You can see that, can't you?"

"In part, but I can't see why you had to be so specific with Mr. Bobbs."

"How do you mean?"

"Was it necessary to your investigation to tell him I'd had not one but two drinks at noon? He already felt I was holding the utility company up to public ridicule by being out of bed on my sick day. But by having two drinks at an hour when decent people are only consuming tea, I moved into the category of a wicked woman, a wicked woman he employed."

Wescott laughed. "I am sorry. But let me assure you that that is solely your Mr. Bobbs's designation. The sheriff's department of Sonoma County does not list you among the ladies of questionable reputation." He leaned back in his chair. "I guess there's nothing I can say now except tell you I'm sorry for the problems this has caused you."

I hesitated. The apology came too suddenly, too easily. I needed more of a battle to sate my anger. But, logically, I got what I asked for, and probably any apology from a sheriff was a victory. "Okay," I said.

"Good." He smiled. "As long as you're here, there is some background information I'd like to get from you. Do you have a few minutes?"

"I have two days."

He hesitated, looking just a bit taken aback. "I can still offer you some of that coffee. Of course, it'll taste even worse by now."

"I'll pass."

"Wise." He leaned against the back of the chair

so that it looked as if it were on the verge of tipping. In the bright fluorescent light, I noticed his eyes—blue, but clearer, sharper, and a bit lighter than the furniture around him. They gave the observer the illusion of looking deep into the depths of his soul.

"So," he said, "tell me about yourself."

His smile, I realized, was like Frank's, an open yet very personal expression. It had done wonders for Frank.

"Where would you like me to start?"

"You came from San Francisco, right? How long ago was that?"

"A little over a year. I got here just before the flooding last year. It wasn't a bad flood then, not like this year's should be, but it was enough to encourage me to buy a house on high ground."

"Why did you move here?" He had a pad propped between his desk and lap and, almost unobtrusively, he took notes.

"I liked the area."

"And?"

"I wanted to move out of the city."

"Why was that?"

"I felt I needed a change."

He put the pad on the desk. "Is this making you nervous?"

"Well, it's not putting me at ease."

"I can set it aside. This isn't an interrogation. I just find it convenient to jot down something I want to come back to; then I can concentrate on what you're saying now. You see?"

I nodded.

"I lived in L.A. before coming here, so I do understand the lure of the area." He leaned back in

the chair again, picked up the pen, and glanced at
me for compliance.

Regardless of the reasons for the notes being
taken, the process did make me edgy, but I felt
foolish objecting. After all, I had nothing to con-
ceal. "Okay," I said. "I'll give you a synopsis. I'm
thirty-two years old. Originally I'm from the East.
I lived in San Francisco for six years and worked
in public relations. I married an account executive
at the company. We had a superb apartment and
made a fair amount of money. We were on the
way up."

"*And then,* if that doesn't sound too melodra-
matic?" He had put down the pen.

"And then," I said, "then it seemed to collapse
from the inside. I can't tell you what happened
first. John and I divorced, but that was the out-
come, not the beginning. I think the beginning was
that I could never leave the bed unmade or the
coffee cups on the table. What I mean is that the
apartment was never mine or even ours. Nothing
was. Our lives were devoted to rising in the company. We spent our money entertaining, dressing
appropriately, buying the right this or that. I never
knew when it would be advantageous for me to
bring a client home or for John to, so the apartment always had to be spotless. It wasn't our
home; it was just an adjunct to our jobs. As we
were. I came to that conclusion; John didn't." I
looked up at Wescott, feeling a bit embarrassed
and rather amazed that I had told him so much
about my divorce. It wasn't something I discussed
anymore. "It's hardly an original story. And probably more than you wanted to know."

"No. There's never more than I want to know."

Over the blue plexiglass partition, I could hear two women discussing Line Q errors on the computer printout.

"Anyway," I said, "I stayed on at work in the city for a while after the divorce, and then I realized I needed to get away. I thought I would come here. I thought I would be moving to a simpler life, a life among wholesome country people. In honor of this metamorphosis, I changed my name from Veronica Joan to Vejay and bought a pickup. The pickup was sensible."

"And not the name?"

I laughed. "Frank kept telling me changing my name was adolescent. Maybe it was. But by that time Vejay was what people called me."

"And did you find peace in the country, Vejay?"

"That sounds like a sappy song title—'Peace in the Country.'"

"Well?" He shrugged off a look of embarrassment.

"I found exactly what you would expect. Instead of down-home folk sitting around the stove at the country store, there were other emigrants from the city searching for the country store. But life here is easier. People are nice. I like my job, and I like the fact that it ends at five."

"Did you think this would be a good place to marry and raise a family?"

"Maybe. I don't know."

"You dated Frank Goulet when you first came here?"

I drew in a breath slowly, seeing clearly where the line of questions was leading. "So this is an interrogation."

"Hardly. Just questions, background." But

there was a steeliness to his voice that had been
absent before. And when I said nothing, he added,
"You were the last person to see Goulet alive."

"The second to last," I reminded him.

"Second," he said. "About your relationship
with Goulet . . ."

His expression remained unchanged, but instead of the spontaneous interest it appeared to
hold a minute before, his face now looked like a
mask held in place by nothing but discipline. It
was the facade of interest John and I used to use
with clients, listening for hours to the expansion
plans of West Coast Metal Pipe or Alvin's Fancy
Pickles, trying to figure how much we could get
out of them for a p.r. campaign. That was one of
the things that had gnawed at me. I wondered
how a client would feel if he found out. Now I
knew—furious and humiliated.

"Look," I said, "if you're going to treat me like
a suspect I'd rather you do it under a bare bulb. I
don't need this pseudo-friend routine."

He drew back visibly. After a pause, he said,
"Okay. Have it your way. You saw Goulet yesterday. You left mad. Now I want to know about
your relationship with him. Clear enough?"

"I dated Frank when I first came to town. A
year ago. Frank dated every new woman. You can
check on that."

"We will."

"I went out with him two or three times. It was
nothing serious, nothing to base the rest of my life
on, to answer your question."

"I didn't ask that specifically. But you did go
out a few times?"

"Probably three."

"Probably?"

"Probably because a few times we ran into each other in town and had coffee. The point is there was never anything between us."

He wrote something on his pad. I could see the small tight marks, but I couldn't read it upside down. He held the pen poised against the pad when he looked up.

"Why did you stop dating?"

"We eased off and stopped, because, as I told you, it was never a big thing. So its ending wasn't very important. I had to go back to the city for a couple of weekends straight to settle business. And then Frank was seeing someone else. And we were just friends. Which is all we ever were."

"Perhaps you were jealous to come back and find Goulet dating another woman?"

I forced myself to take a breath before answering. All my fury that he had so skillfully dissipated by his facade of interest was back. It was an effort to keep from shouting. Yet as angry as I was, I was scared too. Scared for the first time. He was not ruling me out as a suspect. I could hardly believe it. Until this very moment I had always believed that the police, and the sheriff, were there to protect me. I was a white, middle-class, thirtyish woman: exactly the type of person the police look after. With the exception of speeding it had never occurred to me to break a law. But Wescott was not dismissing me. He had realized my vulnerability and made use of it, like he'd do with any murder suspect.

I said, "I was not jealous over Frank. I'm not seventeen. I've been married and divorced. I've been dating for nearly twenty years. I don't view a couple of movies and a dinner as a pledge of life-time devotion. And had it been, I don't know that I would have wanted it."

"What about the woman you assumed Goulet was talking to on the phone? You were mad enough about that to stalk out of the bar."

"I was . . ." I took another breath and started again, calmer. It was one of those things they taught me in "executive school": never let the client get you rattled, or at least never let him know he's got you. "I think I explained that yesterday. Is there anything else you wanted to ask me?"

"Not now." He stood up.

But I remained seated. I didn't want to leave him with nothing but my life to ponder. "You said I was the last person at Frank's. The Chinese Laundry truck was there when I left. Have you checked with them?"

He sat back down. "We have only your word for that."

"Ask the old people across the street. They're famous for spotting any unusual activity on South Bank Road."

"We did. They didn't see a laundry truck."

"What?"

He waited.

"Did you check with the laundry? The laundry must have records." Panic was beginning to be evident in my voice.

"We're checking."

"What about drugs?"

He picked up the pen and leaned toward me. "How do you mean?"

"Suppose Frank was a middleman or someone wanted him to be."

"Do you have information you want to give me on that?"

I wished I did. "Well, no. I just wanted to raise the speculation. There are plenty of drugs around here. It's not unreasonable to think Frank might have been involved in trafficking drugs. I mean, even the authorities admit they can't keep up with the marijuana growers to the north, that they just burn their fields for show."

"Your point, Miss Haskell."

"There are a lot of drugs going through Henderson, and as a bartender and owner, Frank was in a good position to distribute them."

"Do you have anything to indicate that he was?"

"No."

"Any reason for suspicion?"

"Only that he was killed."

He sighed. "You can rest assured that we at the sheriff's department are aware of the drug traffic, perhaps even more aware than you. You may assume that we give it serious consideration in any crime of this nature."

I stood up.

"For the record, Miss Haskell, is there anything more you can tell me?"

"No."

"I assume you will keep yourself available," he said.

"I'll have a lot of free time, at least for the next three days."

I walked out quickly, looking at neither the man at the desk nor the wanted posters. Once outside I felt relieved, as if I'd escaped. But my stomach still churned with the midnight terrors. Less than twenty-four hours ago I was a normal, middle-class woman. Since then I had been suspended from my job—a matter that now seemed almost trivial—and the sheriff suspected me of murdering a man.

As I walked to the pickup I shifted back to thinking that surely he couldn't envision me as a murderer, surely this questioning was just for show, surely . . . but it wasn't. He manipulated me as he would any suspect.

And from what I knew of this type of investigation (learned mainly from prime-time police shows), I suspected that the sheriff would focus on his best lead until something better was presented to him. In other words, he was going to concentrate on me.

By the time I left the sheriff's department, the air was thick with the threat of rain and the sky was dark, though it was just a bit after four.

I considered driving into Santa Rosa. Probably the Chinese Laundry was there, but I wasn't sure. I also wasn't sure the hand launderers would speak English. Probably not. And I had purposely avoided the laundry truck at Frank's Place. So even if the driver had noticed Frank, he wouldn't know whether that was before or after I was there.

I shifted the pickup into reverse and backed out. The Chinese Laundry could wait till tomorrow. Better I should concentrate on what and who might have caused Frank's death.

I turned onto North Bank Road toward Henderson. Live oaks hung over the road from both sides. Even at midday the pavement was shaded by a wonderfully verdant canopy. I loved this section of road.

Frank, I thought. He wanted to get out of San Francisco, and he'd heard about Henderson from Chris Fortimiglio, so he came here and bought the bar and ran it for two years, until he was shot. That left a lot of questions. Why did Frank want to leave the city? Had I asked him? I couldn't remember doing so. No. When he mentioned wanting to leave, it seemed natural to me, since I had left. But Frank could have had more pressing reasons than a change of scenery. Still, he had enough money to buy, or at least put a down payment on, the Place. So he wasn't leaving the city because of bad debts or anything like that. And Henderson was too close to the city, with too many city people coming back and forth, for Frank to consider hiding out here—particularly in a job as visible as tending bar.

Whatever his reasons for leaving San Francisco, they couldn't have been too pressing. Still, it wouldn't hurt to know more about them.

But if the motivation behind Frank's murder wasn't something in San Francisco, then it must be here. I recalled the conversation at the Fortimiglios' the night before—was it that recent? Madge Oombs said if the killer couldn't have been a stranger trotting down South Bank Road for all the world to see, then it must have been someone local, slipping in along the river.

Then, too, the cause must have been something local. What? What had Frank done in his two years here? He ran the bar. And? Well, he dated a lot of women, but most of them were tourists, who would see him as a summer fling. Even if they hoped for more, it was unlikely that they would arrive one afternoon in flood season and shoot Frank in the forehead.

Of course, he dated local women, but not many. The only one I could think of who had even been speculatively linked with him was Patsy Fernandez, and I felt sure there was no truth to that rumor. She and Paul were too close. Surely. Well, pretty surely. Of course, Paul and Patsy were from

San Francisco. Could they have known Frank there? I should find out about that.

If the cause was not women, what about men?

A truck passed me and cut in front of me, missing my bumper by inches. I hit the horn, but by that time the truck was yards ahead of me. Glancing at the speedometer, I saw that I was driving twenty-five miles an hour. The speed limit here was fifty-five, and few drivers observed that. I stepped on the gas.

But Frank and men; Frank gay? It seemed impossible. If he had been gay, he had been hiding in the back of his closet. Considering the growing gay population in the Russian River area, there would have been no advantage in pretending to be straight, and such deception would have created plenty of resentment in the gay world.

A sports car swerved around me. I was doing thirty-five. Obviously, I could think or I could drive, not both. I pushed down on the accelerator and turned the radio on, loud.

By the time I got to Henderson it was raining in earnest. I pulled up in front of Thompson's grocery. The sidewalk was raised here, up two steps from the street. Puddles from the last few days of rain surrounded it. I jumped from the truck to a dry spot four feet from the curb and walked twenty feet along the road before I found a narrow enough stretch of water to leap over.

In Thompson's I bought a can of beef stew (inability to cook was one of my business executive attributes that stuck with me) and a bottle of brandy. But as I made my way back to the pickup, I realized that even heating the stew was more than I felt like doing. I put the bag in the cab and walked across the street to the café.

I was not hungry when I was here for breakfast, but now I was starved. Perhaps fear burned calories. One of the café's fine qualities was their menu —it offered all kinds of food at any time of the day. That, I believe, had been forced upon them by the sewer laborers who usually wanted what was normally considered dinner at seven in the morning. Now, at four-thirty, I ordered scrambled eggs, sausage, and sauerkraut.

I sat in the same secluded corner I was in this morning, propped a discarded newspaper in front of me to discourage conversation, and returned to thoughts of Frank. If he wasn't killed because of his social life, then why? What had he been doing at the Place to necessitate someone killing him?

I pondered that till the eggs arrived, but I came up with no more reasonable speculation than that Frank was involved in drugs. When I suggested that to Sheriff Wescott, I was merely tossing out the first thing on my mind to distract him from me. But now, considering it, with a mouth full of sauerkraut, it made a good deal of sense. There were a lot of drugs in this area. Marijuana was the biggest cash crop in Humboldt County to the north, and Humboldt was a large county. Each autumn the authorities (combinations of local, state, and federal), surveyed the area from helicopters, sprayed paraquat, and burned fields. They watched the roads for suspicious vehicles heading toward San Francisco, Berkeley, and beyond to Los Angeles. But, as I smugly pointed out to Wescott, that was all for show. So many people were involved with marijuana in one way or another that any effort to eradicate it was useless.

Suppose Frank had been involved in dealing, maybe in a minor way, when he lived in San Francisco? Suppose he had a source north of here? Suppose he had found out that he could run a profitable way station at the Place—that suppliers could bring the weed there, either for Frank to distribute to smaller dealers in the area or in larger quantity to "tourists" from the city? Suppose Frank had gotten greedy, or one of his suppliers or customers did? That would make sense. Frank wouldn't have had any qualms about dealing drugs, at least not recreational drugs. Marijuana was the most likely contraband because of the location, though, I supposed, he might have arranged for cocaine to be smuggled off a ship in the ocean and up the Russian River. I'd have to ask Chris about that possibility.

When I finished my eggs I felt better than I had all afternoon. Drugs made a lot of sense. And the people who had been involved in the drug scene, who had been in San Francisco, and who had access to boats, were Patsy and Paul Fernandez.

It was just after five. The rain was heavy now. As I crossed the bridge I looked over the railing to check the height of the river, but it was too dark to make out anything.

South Bank Road was lower than the bridge and I turned west onto it. Paul and Patsy's canoe rental was half a mile away.

The road was dark. Houses and businesses were locked, with flood preparations made and the owners gone. The water had saturated lawns on either side of the road, and it wouldn't be long before the road itself would be inundated.

The canoe rental was located in what once had been a large wooden barn. In summer the canoes were either at the dock or on the main floor there. Now they were suspended from the sloping roof like oblong chandeliers above the muddy dirt floor. The only dry area was the raised wooden platform behind the counter and the storeroom in the rear.

I pulled up by the storeroom door. The Fernandez' old VW van was gone, which meant Patsy wasn't home yet. She worked, in some clerical capacity, at Solano Construction, the company that was laying the sewer pipe. It wouldn't be long till she arrived.

I knocked. "Paul?"

In a minute he opened the door.

"Oh, Vejay. Well, come in."

I held out the paper bag (minus the beef stew). "I thought I might convince you guys to share some brandy."

Paul smiled. "I'd say that was a safe guess. Come on in. Have a seat while I pour. Patsy shouldn't be too long." He was shouting. Music, heavy on drums and horns, came from speakers in opposite corners of the small room. Paul turned down the volume on his way to the sink.

The room resembled nothing so much as the back room at PG&E except that while the other was tan, this was boat gray. Like the PG&E room, these walls were covered with metal cases holding mysterious metal objects of odd shapes and unknown purposes, presumably canoe stuff. As a storeroom it might have been satisfactory, but as a home it was awful. And while Paul and Patsy had added a leather sofa, an oriental rug, the elaborate stereo, and a television, the effect did not convert the room into a home, but only cluttered the storage room.

Still, it was warm. Gargantuan space heaters occupied the two free corners, making the room more comfortable than any place I'd been in this month—certainly cozier than my house.

I took one of the filled brandy glasses from Paul and sat on the leather ottoman.

"What have you been up to?" he asked, settling on the sofa.

"I've been suspended from work and interviewed twice by the sheriff. How's that for starters?"

"Suspended? How come?"

"My boss doesn't believe I was sick yesterday."

"Well, what business is that of his? You have sick leave, don't you? What is he, a doctor or something?" Paul leaned forward, almost propelled off the sofa by his indignation.

I took a sip of my brandy, thinking that I liked Paul.

"Mr. Bobbs, my boss, feels it's obvious to the community as a whole that I wasn't sick, and he doesn't want PG&E to look foolish."

"What's your union doing? They shouldn't put up with that."

"The union? I completely forgot about them. It just happened this afternoon. And then I charged down to the sheriff's office."

Paul pulled back the slightest bit. It was apparent that while being suspended from work was a very acceptable circumstance for a friend, going to the sheriff's office of one's own volition was definitely suspect.

"Sheriff Wescott told my boss that I'd had two drinks at Frank's. I figured that was not the type of information he ought to be passing on. So I went to tell him that."

"Chewed him out, huh? How'd he take that? I'll bet they don't get a lot of lip here, these sheriffs. Well, good for you. Told them where to get off, huh? Here, let me get you some more brandy."

I hadn't finished what I had, but I let Paul refill the glass. Which question should I ask Paul first? I wanted to take advantage of the glow of the brandy and the camaraderie we were sharing over my supposed tongue-lashing of the sheriff.

"It seems odd none of us ever saw each other in San Francisco," I said as Paul settled back onto the sofa.

"Big place."

"I suppose. Still, you get around. You lived in the Haight, didn't you?"

"Uh-huh."

"What did you do there? I mean, you obviously didn't rent canoes."

He laughed. "There were plenty of people high enough that I could have *sold* them canoes. If they'd had money. That was the problem. That's always the problem. Just like it is here. Cash flow."

I didn't want to let Paul get onto his finances. "But what *did* you do there?"

"A little of this, a little of that."

"Like delivering flyers?"

"Yeah, that and collecting. Collecting was a big thing. Activists, they called us, as if we were devoted to whatever cause it was. The only thing that interested us was the couple of bucks an hour. The people who cared about health centers and sea mammals were in the offices; they weren't tramping door to door."

"But how could you survive like that? I mean, surely that wasn't steady work?"

"We weren't living on Nob Hill! Patsy and me, we know how to make money stretch. We don't live high." He gestured toward the room.

I smiled. "Did you know Frank then?"

"Frank Goulet? No. There's no way we would have been in the same circles as he was."

"Why do you say that?"

"You just know to look at him. He never lived with six other people in a room. You can tell he always had his own clothes."

I sipped my brandy to hide a smile. I'd never considered owning your own clothes a status symbol.

"Frank," Paul continued, "had to have had money. I mean he bought Frank's Place. You don't do that without big bucks."

"But you never saw him in the Haight, never heard about him dealing drugs?"

Another time, with less brandy, with someone who had not berated the sheriff, Paul might have become suspicious. But now he leaned back against the sofa and considered the possibility. "No. I'm sure I would have recognized him here if I'd seen him before. But that doesn't mean he wasn't doing drugs there."

"Do you know if he did any here?"

"You mean used, or dealt?"

"Either."

He shrugged, pushed himself up, and headed for the bottle, giving me a questioning glance on the way. I shook my head.

"Everyone uses, don't they? Do you know anyone who doesn't at least smoke weed?"

He had his back to me, so I could ignore the question.

"But dealing? If he did, I didn't hear about it. But Patsy knew Frank better than I did. You can ask her."

It was nearly quarter to six. "Shouldn't she be home soon?" I asked.

"Should be here now. Maybe she stopped at the store."

We sat in silence, which seemed fine with Paul. He listened to the stereo and drank my brandy. I sat and sloshed the brandy around the glass.

"Are your canoes all up?" I asked.

"Every last one."

"You haven't had any stolen, or borrowed and returned, have you?"

"No." He sat up, suspicious. "Why?"

"You remember Madge Oombs saying Frank's killer could have come by river."

"In my canoe!"

"No one else rents canoes on the river, do they?"

"No. I checked that before we took the lease here. I wasn't going to deal with competition. You get too many guys doing the same thing and it can kill you."

"So none of your canoes could have been missing? Would you be sure to know if they had been?"

"Every canoe here has its place. I check them

each night and morning. People steal things. Kids try for free rides. I'm no fool. I keep good track of these canoes." He swallowed the rest of his brandy and stood up.

As he passed the door, it opened and Patsy walked in.

"Is that brandy?" she asked. "I can sure use a glass. I've had a—"

Before she could finish her sentence Paul wrapped an arm around her shoulder and kissed her. When she emerged, she was looking toward me. She seemed surprised.

"Vejay, what are you doing here?"

"Just sharing some brandy." Even in the rain she should have seen my pickup parked outside. "I've been here a while, as you can tell from the bottle. I thought you would be home sooner."

"Well, I . . . paperwork. Sometimes you just don't get it done. And nothing is so vital as paperwork. When you work part-time, they really raise a stink if everything's not done."

"Vejay got suspended," Paul announced, handing Patsy a glass. "Then she went and chewed out the sheriff."

I could see that these accomplishments were considerably less impressive to the sober listener. And even I didn't have enough interest to recount them once more. I said, "We were just speculating about Frank. Maybe his death was somehow connected with drugs."

When she didn't say anything, I prompted, "What do you think?"

"I don't know. Why would I know?"

"I thought you might have heard of Frank when you were living in San Francisco."

"No."

"Paul said you might know if he did any dealing here."

She glared at Paul, then at me. "He didn't. I wouldn't know. I've had a rotten day and I'm in a rotten mood and this isn't making it any better. I'm tired of people asking me about Frank. It's really infuriating, for me and for Paul. Frank could have been selling land on the moon for all I know."

"I just thought you might have heard something about him dealing marijuana. It wouldn't be unknown for a bartender to deal drugs."

"I left the drug scene in the city. I don't know who deals what here. I just go to work and rent canoes."

I stood to leave.

"And you know, Vejay," Patsy added, "I don't like all this pawing over Frank's life. He's dead. Don't you care? Or are you just interested in seeing what kind of slime you can stir up?"

I started to answer, to defend myself, but I could see Patsy's eyes brimming. So I kept my mouth shut, nodded to Paul, and slunk out.

It was well I had restrained myself from drinking more brandy. The parking lot outside Paul and Patsy's was dark and wet; it would be hard to avoid its many potholes. Patsy's van was about ten feet from me. She must indeed have had a rotten day to have overlooked my truck.

Had my questions been abrupt to the point of rudeness? Had the brandy and Paul's unsuspicious responses smothered my usual caution? Or had I hit a raw spot?

I backed the truck slowly and pulled out of the

parking lot, hitting only two potholes. South Bank Road was still above water, but one acacia leaned heavily and it was unlikely to survive another day.

I crossed the bridge and hit the red light at the end. I was still thinking of Patsy and Frank, and of Frank and drugs, as I came to the turn for my house. I hesitated, knowing from ample experience that the house, which would have been cold at five, would be icy now. There was not enough time before bed to get it anywhere near warm.

I turned left into town.

I might have had Skip Bollo in the back of my mind. I don't know. But when I saw the light on in his real estate office, I stopped.

CHAPTER

8

Henderson Realty was in the center of a short block of shops and offices built within the last ten years and raised well above the street level. There was a double walkway: one sidewalk at the normal level by the street, and a wooden walk four feet above that. In front of each shop eight steps connected the two. The shops were shingled and tasteful without being too cute. Skip Bollo had had a hand in the building of the block. It should have been a good investment.

I climbed the steps, stood for a moment under the overhang, shaking the rain from my slicker, then walked in.

Skip Bollo was sitting behind the last of three desks. The office was carpeted in a caramel brown that, as I recalled from a psychology class, was a color that people instinctively connect with home and security. The walls were beige, the furniture solid and substantial, and the large potted plants green and healthy. It was the office of a man whom you'd trust.

"Hi, Skip," I said.

He pushed his file drawer shut and stood up. "This is a surprise. Are you panicking and do you want to sell your house?"

"No. I saw your light on." I walked back and sat in the seat next to his desk as he settled back in

his chair. I could tell he wondered why I was here
—a natural reaction, since I hadn't been in this
office after I'd bought my house from him—but he
was too polite to ask.

Putting the papers in front of him in a folder, he
said, "Your visit is a welcome excuse to interrupt
work." In spite of the hour and his being alone, he
was still wearing a herringbone jacket. It fit well
and looked comfortable. The gray of the fabric
picked up the gray of his hair and accented his
slate blue eyes. His skin was hardly wrinkled, his
features chiseled. But his nose was what one first
noticed. It was a cartoonlike bulb, too big for his
face. Knowing Skip, this was not the nose he
would have chosen for himself. But it was this appealing imperfection that made him seem immediately likable. Without it, he would have looked
too precise, finicky, bordering on the homosexual
stereotype. The nose, more than anything, may
have been responsible for his success.

I didn't know where to begin. All I could think
of was Skip sitting with Madge Oombs at the restaurant on Route 101 yesterday morning, and I
knew I didn't want to start with that. I asked,
"Has the sheriff talked to you about Frank's
death?"

"No. Should he have?"

"I suppose that does seem an odd question.
Since he's talked to me twice I just assume that
he's made the rounds of everyone in town. It's not
a good thing to be the last one to see a man alive."

"Have they been bothering you?" He seemed
truly concerned. It was the same feeling I'd had
about him when he went through seven or eight
houses with me before I decided on mine.

"Wescott isn't hassling me. But he hasn't ruled me out either. I'm just continually startled that he could suspect me at all."

Skip smiled sadly. "It's always disappointing when someone prejudges you."

I hesitated to acknowledge his statement. While there had been anti-gay feeling lately, Skip had been here for years. Still, he was different; "homosexual, but quite nice," was how he had been described to me early on. "I guess you've been prejudged here?" I said.

"It was always subtle until the last couple years." He stared past me out the picture window that formed the front of the office. The rain was coming down hard, enveloping us in the warm dry office. There were none of the usual night sounds —no auto horns beeping, no tires skidding, no doors slamming, no voices calling back and forth. It was as if we were totally alone.

He said, "I came to Henderson ten years ago. No one around here thought about homosexuals then. Gays were people who lived in San Francisco and dressed oddly. They weren't men who opened the real estate offices in Henderson. It was quite a while before anyone questioned my preferences. I try to be courteous—I don't try to hide my life, but I don't want to rub it in anyone's face either. It was nice, those years and the ones after. It was nice just being a realtor. Seven, eight years. You're not a minority until there are enough of you to be noticed. And that started happening only recently."

"But," I said, "you're still not totally accepted. Not 'normal.'"

He sat forward, seeming to shake off his intro-

spective mood. "No, not normal. But that was
fine. Had I desired normality, I would have married, had children, and lived in Pleasant Hill."

"Tell me," I said, searching for the right entree.
"How did you see Frank?" That certainly wasn't
it. "I mean, you knew Frank as well as the rest of
us, but there was apparently some facet of Frank
which none of us suspected, something that led to
his being killed. . . ."

"Possibly. It's also conceivable that some lunatic wandered in, demanded a drink in the afternoon, and when Frank refused, shot him."

"If so, he came unobserved. Like Madge said."

"True. It's stretching a point to think a lunatic
stole a canoe, paddled down the river at this time
of year, and came up through Frank's trap door
just to demand a drink."

"And then paddled back upstream!"

The wind hurled a sheet of water against the
window. We both started and turned, relieved to
see the window still in place.

"I'm afraid, Vejay, that I can't tell you anything
new about Frank. No esoteric observations. He
was just a nice enough guy who had the sense to
buy a bar in a good location, make a few inexpen-
sive improvements like adding a fireplace and getting Rosa to bring in those wonderful dinners, and
he had himself a going business. If he was involved
in something more, it was a shame. He should
have been satisfied. What he had would have satisfied most men."

"But it didn't satisfy Frank, did it?"

Skip propped his fingertips against their mates.
"Presumably not."

"Why not? What was there in Frank that left

him, well, unfulfilled? What kept Frank from being a happy bar owner?"

"I don't know. Maybe you'd better talk to a psychiatrist rather than a realtor, Vejay."

I laughed. "I'm beginning to think that's not a bad idea. But for the moment, you're all I have. You're not pressed for time now, are you?" I asked as an afterthought. He had been working when I barged in; Skip, a firm believer in courtesy, might find it lacking in me.

"No. The windows are shuttered at my house. The plants are covered, and there's no danger of flooding that high up. I've done everything I can. And here," he smiled, "well, no one's going to be buying real estate during a flood. No, I'm not busy. If Frank were alive I'd be at Frank's Place."

"What was Frank like when he was buying the Place? He bought it from you, didn't he?"

"Had no choice. I was the only realtor in town then."

"Rosa said that Frank came up here, spent about a week, and the next thing they knew he bought the place. He must have been a model client for you."

"He was. He knew what he wanted. He asked about bars, and, I think, restaurants. There weren't many for sale. There never are at any one time. It's a small area. I showed him the write-ups on a couple places, and he chose the Place."

"What was it that appealed to him?"

Skip sat, absently massaging his left forefinger. "I didn't give that any thought. I don't when someone is definite. It doesn't make any difference then. I only try to figure it out when a person is unsure."

"Like I was?"

"Well, Vejay, it was your first house. Of course, it was a hard decision. When a woman buys her first house she wants it to be perfect, and perfection is rare."

"But you did try to narrow down what I wanted?"

He leaned forward with that worldly, amused look of his. "After I see a client go through two or three houses and still appear confused, I make an effort—you won't be offended now if I reveal a trade secret, will you?"

I shook my head.

"I categorize them. There are the socially mobile people who want a house to stun their friends. They're the ones who would choose a deck above indoor plumbing. Then there are the opposites, the convenience-oriented. But most of them prefer Santa Rosa. They'd only live along the river if they had to. Then they'd be so angry at their fate they'd demand their house make up for it."

"And what was I?" I could tell from his expression that my question had created a dilemma for a courteous person. "It's okay, Skip, I won't be offended."

Still, he looked hesitant. "You were, well, a recent divorcee."

"How nineteen-thirties!"

"You said you wouldn't be offended."

"I'm not. Go on."

"It's not uncommon for people who have been through a divorce, particularly if it's unpleasant, to want nothing to do with their former life. They want a house that's entirely different, something that would offend their former spouses. They don't really *want* anything; they just know what they *don't* want."

I smiled. It was true, but it had taken me a long time to realize it. "You found me that house."

"Another secret?"

"Yes. Tell me."

"I tricked you."

"You what?"

"You would have been as happy in any of the houses you went through before. But with this one, I told you it was a house some people from the city had hated."

I laughed and felt all the tension of the day bubbling out. "I remember that. They were not only city people, they were public relations people— what I had been. You knew that, didn't you?"

"Probably. I don't remember any more. You're not angry, are you? Normally, I would never mention this."

"No. You did the right thing. At that time I could have tramped through every house in town and still been dissatisfied. And my house is wonderful. But how come you categorized me so easily and you couldn't figure out Frank?"

I saw that I had put him in an awkward position. This time I let it stand.

"As I said, I didn't have to make any decision about Frank. He came, he saw the Place, and he wanted it. He was prepared to offer the owner more than the asking price. He wasn't in a hurry about closing escrow. He told me he would consider whatever the owner wanted, just as long as it was aboveboard; he didn't want to discover later that he'd been cheated." Skip shrugged. "No one does, of course, but few are willing to admit to worrying about it. So Frank, in many ways, was a perfect client."

"But what was it about Frank's Place that attracted him?"

"I can't be sure. Perhaps it was its history during Prohibition. That's when the trap door was added. The owners dug a sort of well at the end of the little inlet under the trap door. When the Feds came, they would lower the liquor down into the well. When the coast was clear they'd hoist it up. Frank liked that. He even considered calling the Place the Speakeasy."

"But he didn't."

"Rightly, I think. He decided that name was too cute."

The rain was still slamming down. If anything it seemed to be falling harder. Skip hadn't given me a new insight into Frank's character, but I couldn't think of anything else to ask about except the drugs. "Did Frank ever mention drugs?"

"Everyone mentions drugs."

"Do you think Frank could have been dealing?"

"Vejay, I don't know. Anyone could. You could. I don't pry into people's business. I just sell their houses."

That, I thought, sounded very much like Patsy, telling me to butt out. Awkwardly, I said, "I guess houses are selling pretty well now."

Skip followed the change of subject gladly. "There's been a lot of turnover in the last year or so. Even considering that the sewer project is two years behind schedule, people are still buying. Businesses are selling. Sellers are enthusiastic about the two-year lease-options." Skip was becoming enthusiastic.

"Two-year options?"

"It's a great deal for a seller. Maybe you should consider it, Vejay. The way it works is that the buyer pays for option rights and makes the monthly lease payments for two years. Real estate prices in this area will skyrocket as soon as the sewer is in, so you can get a good price for the option. And if at the end of the two years the buyer can't exercise the option, or chooses not to, you can lease it or sell it again. I've sold a couple of commercial pieces for the second time."

"Why commercial?"

"You know about the ordinance that bans new businesses opening until the sewer is hooked up, don't you?"

"Yes. Oh. So businessmen bought, assuming the sewer would be completed, and when it wasn't, they had no business, right?"

"Right. Larger companies could have afforded the payment, but they preferred to let the property go and take the tax loss. It works with homes, too, though not so dramatically. It's a little different." He was assessing me.

"I'll pass, Skip. I like my house too much to gamble with it." And I didn't care for the idea of luring someone else to lose their investment. It seemed discourteous. Apparently Skip saw it otherwise. I wondered how much he compartmentalized his values. Perhaps he just felt that adult people could take care of themselves.

It was still raining hard. The front window was completely steamed. I hated the thought of going back out, but I couldn't find a reason to stay longer. I reached for the doorknob, then turned back to Skip Bollo. "Oh, by the way, I almost said hello to you and Madge at the restaurant on 101 yesterday morning."

He didn't say anything, but his startled expression that quickly shifted from fear to annoyance told me I was not about to get an explanation of that tête-à-tête. I said quickly, "Patsy seems very upset about Frank's death."

Ignoring my non sequitur, Skip picked up on the offered diversion. "They were friends. I used to see them around town. Sometimes in the state park. I . . . Look, Vejay, I do have some work. I . . ."

"Sure, Skip, I've kept you a long time."

This time I did leave, wondering what it was that Skip had discussed with Madge that made him so uncomfortable.

What Skip Bollo had told me most about was myself. And of Frank? Either Skip knew nothing or was willing to admit nothing about drugs. But something about the Place was exactly what Frank wanted. What? I understood the bar in there before Frank had done a decent business. It was owned by an old couple and sold when they grew too decrepit to operate it. Still, Frank didn't buy the name from them. He wasn't buying good will. The location was pleasant, but for a bar, in town would have been a better location. Had Frank, as Skip suggested, fallen in love with the Place's history—the Prohibition-era speakeasy with liquor stowed in the inlet beneath the trap door? If so, he hadn't made any visible use of it in the operation of the Place. But perhaps the attraction was more than cosmetic. A trap door would be very useful to a drug dealer.

I raced the engine, forcing the heater higher. It occurred to me that I was spending a lot of time lately sitting in my truck with the engine idling. It was nine o'clock. I was pleased with my conclusion. It was so logical. I was ready to shift into reverse and drive on home when it struck me that logical though a drug motive might be, I had not one bit of evidence, a number of loose ends, and no suspects.

I raced the engine again.

What I needed was some proof that Frank had had marijuana in the Place. Had the police swept it out, looking for leaves, for stems, for seeds? Wescott hadn't mentioned it, but he wouldn't have. And Frank might not have had his contraband stash behind the bar or in a spot immediately noticeable. He would have had it hidden, some place near the trap door.

I tried to picture Frank with other customers. Had he ever behaved strangely, left the room and returned carrying a bag or box? I couldn't recall anything odd. Still, it was the Place he wanted, so he had to be keeping the drugs there. Surely if I had thought of this, Wescott would have. That is, if he wasn't concentrating only on me.

But short of breaking into the Place, there was nothing I could do.

What else had Skip told me? He'd seen Frank with Patsy Fernandez in town and in the state park. Patsy had certainly reacted strongly to my questions. She'd been upset last night at Rosa's. It was one thing to run into Frank downtown. I'd done that myself any number of times. But the state park was something else. The nearest entrance was halfway to Guerneville. It was a place you had to drive to, a place you went to for a reason, to commune with nature, or to meet without half the town knowing about it. It was, in a way, equivalent to the restaurant on Route 101.

And *that* was the main thing Skip had told me. Whatever he had discussed with Madge that morning was definitely something he didn't want known.

I put the truck in reverse and backed into the street. Madge lived in one of the little houses on the hill behind town. I'd been there only once, and I wasn't at all sure I could find it on a dark, rainy night. I turned left, circled through town, and looped back onto North Bank Road, past Madge's antique shop. A dim light was visible through the steamy front window. With relief, I pulled up in front.

CHAPTER
9

Unlike Skip's sensibly situated, carefully decorated office, Madge Oombs's antique shop was on the river side of North Bank Road. And rather than being eight safe steps up, it slumped in the mud beside the road. The shop was old, its wooden frame denuded of any paint, and warped by years of exposure to rain. The front window was always in need of a wash; inside, the "antiques" were either stacked on top of tables or piled under them, thrust into corners or clumped wherever they could be squeezed in. A dust rag was an unknown commodity to Madge.

The few times I'd been there, Madge had been sitting on one or another of the pieces of merchandise, reading. In old boots, jeans, a plaid shirt, and, frequently, a bandana, she looked like she'd been cleaning the attic and had just stopped to take a rest.

Initially I'd wondered how Madge survived. But it took only one tourist season to find out. Tourists accepted her at face value—an unsophisticated woman, anxious to get rid of all this junk. Madge got prices I wouldn't have believed.

I climbed down from the pickup. No doubt Madge was having a glass of wine, reading a novel, and waiting for the flood water to give her shop more atmosphere.

I pushed the door open. Inside, the front table that had held enough carnival glass to keep a Ringling, was empty. Madge was climbing the ladder to the attic, clutching a cardboard box. I watched her balance her sturdy, be-jeaned bottom against the side of the hatch door, and place the box on the attic floor.

Clomping down the stairs, she glared at the glass, china, brass, and crystal that crowded on tables and in cases, then sat down hard on the bottom rung.

"Vejay! I didn't hear you come in. What are you doing out on a night like this? Sit. Look, there's a whole clear table behind you. You can lay out if you want. I've just been carting junk up to the attic. Real pain in the ass. Every year I swear I'll never do it again. When I see the flood coverage on television I ask myself what kind of lunatic is flooded out annually."

Gray-streaked strands of hair escaped from the rubber band at the nape of her neck. As she spoke each breath batted the errant strands away from her mouth. Her face was smudged, her shirt and jeans streaked with dirt. She was not a sight which Skip Bollo would find attractive. It dawned on me that only one thing could have drawn Skip to their morning tête-à-tête.

"You're selling the shop, aren't you?" I blurted out.

She stared a moment, then shot a glance at the attic hole.

"No."

It was a particularly unconvincing no.

"That's what you were talking to Skip about yesterday morning at the truck stop, isn't it?"

Again she looked toward the attic and back to me. "Vejay, what's got into you? You must have been out in the weather too long. What are you walking in here making crazy accusations for?"

"Accusations" was an odd choice of word, I was thinking, when I heard a noise in the attic. I looked up in time to see Rosa's face peer down. "Madge," she called, "come on, now. We don't have all night and you've got twice more than what you had last year. We'll be doing well to get it all up here. Now don't just sit there."

Ignoring me, Madge began to load vases and wine glasses into a box. Rosa's head disappeared.

"You are going to sell," I said to Madge.

"Vejay," she whispered, "you must be forgetting who you're talking to. I've lived in Henderson all my life. I was born here. Rosa and I went to school here. I was married here, both times. I've owned this shop for thirty years." She hoisted the box and climbed up the steps, handing it to Rosa overhead.

Rosa slid the box back from the entryway. Looking down, she called, "Is that you, Vejay?" She poked her head further through the hole. "Have you come to help Madge? That's real nice. We can use all the help we can get. Maybe you can move Madge a little faster down there."

"I'll try, Rosa." So far, I'd succeeded at *that*.

I lifted a cardboard box onto the empty table and began stacking picture frames in it—wooden, brass, and a couple that looked suspiciously like aluminum. When Madge stepped down the ladder the box was nearly full. I gathered up four more small frames, put them in, and whispered to her, "I talked to Skip Bollo just now."

She hesitated.

"The two-year option?"

She didn't reply. She grabbed the box and carried it up.

"You're doing good," Rosa called down to me. "Just keep her moving. I don't know what Madge would do without her friends."

I had another box filled when Madge descended. Without pause she carried it back up.

It was three boxes later that I said, "This is a valuable piece of land. Are you offering it for a commercial complex, with the two-year option?"

She put down the box. "Look, Vejay. I don't like these questions. They're insulting and they're dumb. I'm not offering anything. For one reason, because I love this town and I don't want to see it change. And for another because nobody's buying anything. As long as the sewer is held up, and that could be forever the way things are going, no new businesses or apartments can open, so there's no reason for anyone to buy. Do I have to make that any clearer?"

She hoisted the box and moved quickly up the stairs. Watching her, I realized what a strong woman she was. She must have been packing and climbing for a couple of hours before I arrived, but she showed remarkably little wear. Her broad shoulders and square frame filled the plaid shirt. Madge was one of those self-reliant, pioneer-stock women who came by her muscles through necessity. I suspected she had never bothered with anything so effete as "exercise," but she did chop her own wood, carry her own boxes, and thought nothing of walking all the way into Guerneville.

She was, I realized, a woman who could handle a small boat at flood time.

"Madge," I said, handing her a box of light fixtures, "you . . ."

But she didn't stop, didn't meet my gaze. She took the box and climbed back up. At the attic hole, she said, "Come on, Rosa. It's nearly ten o'clock. Your family will be ready for bed."

"But Madge, we haven't half finished."

"It'll still be here tomorrow."

"So will the flood waters."

"Not tomorrow. You don't hear any frogs, do you?"

Rosa laughed, and in a minute she was climbing down the steps after Madge.

"Frogs?" I asked.

"One of the old-timers' secrets. We know it will flood when the frogs cross North Bank Road and you can hear them croaking at night. You hear any frogs, Vejay?"

"No."

"Not yet, you mean. When you hear them, then it will flood."

With a sigh Rosa sat down on the empty table. In contrast to Madge, she looked drained. "The least you can do is give me a glass of wine before I leave, Madge," she said. "I'll call Carlo to come for me."

"No, you won't," Madge said. "Vejay can drive you. She was just leaving anyway."

I hadn't been planning to leave at all. I'd intended to stay long enough to find out the truth behind Madge's evasions, a plan that was obviously as clear to her as to me. But I had no more desire to discuss Madge's selling out in front of

Rosa than she did. I said, "Of course. I wouldn't be presuming, would I, to think you might have discussed Frank?"

Rosa raised an eyebrow and smiled. "You must think we gossip all the time, Vejay."

"No. I'd find it odd if you hadn't given him some thought. Everyone else has. The sheriff talked to me twice already."

"Twice? You mean after I spoke to him?"

"Once before, once after. I'm afraid your support wasn't enough to make him discount me entirely. Though in fairness I did go in to see him." I recounted my suspension from work and my scene with Wescott. Madge watched me appraisingly; Rosa nodded in agreement with my statements and scowled as I repeated the sheriff's. "So all in all, I'm left with wondering about drugs. What do you think?"

"Frank never said anything about marijuana."

"Rosa, if he were selling drugs, he wouldn't start by telling everyone. It's not a legal activity," Madge said.

"He was at our house for dinner, for lunch. Two, three weeks he stayed with us. There was nothing odd, nothing illegal about anything he did."

I wondered what Frank would have to have done to undermine Rosa's determined faith in him. She was a good friend to have.

"How much did you see Frank, Madge?" I asked.

"Not often. At the bar, at Rosa's, but not much to talk to. I was a little old and tough for Frank's taste." She handed Rosa and me filled wine glasses, but did not put the bottle on the table for refills. "Frank came in here maybe three or four times altogether. There was no reason for him to be here more."

"He stopped in with us before he bought the Place, when he was still staying at our house," Rosa said.

"I remember that. He was one of the few people who wasn't outraged at my prices."

We laughed.

"This is hardly Frank's kind of stuff," Madge said. "But he did know something about jade and ivory. He said he'd recently sold his favorite netsuke—this was almost two years ago. I remember he described it as a carving of three old women standing back to back. One had gold teeth. When you think that netsukes are only about the size of an egg, you can imagine the craftsmanship those teeth required." Madge drained her wine glass. "Frank told me he sold it for five hundred dollars and thought he was getting a good price. When he delivered it, the buyer told him it was worth five thousand! So Frank understood the money there was to be made in art and antiques. It made me kind of uneasy when he started asking me about running the shop."

"Was Frank thinking of opening an antique shop?" Rosa asked.

"I never could decide, Rosa. When he first came in here, right after he moved to Henderson, he asked me a lot of questions about the business, where I got my Depression glass, and my antique frames—some of those really are antique—and the bronze work, and he asked about a couple of buddhas I had then and one painting. I thought he might buy the painting, which would have been a joke, but I was wrong. Afterwards, when I considered it, I felt sure he never intended to buy anything. He was really only interested in how to run the shop. I thought he might be planning to open an antique shop of his own."

"You think so?" Rosa asked.

"Nothing happened for a year and a half, so I forgot it. Then last month Frank came in. He asked me about vacant stores. I can tell you, that put me on edge. Henderson can't support two antique shops. There are enough already along the river close to Guerneville."

"What did you tell him?" I asked.

"Nothing," she said. "He knew the town as well as I did. But I did remind him about the ordinance banning new business licenses until the sewer is installed. So if Frank was thinking of opening a store, it must have been long-range planning."

The building shook. The glass rattled.

"That wind is a bad sign," Rosa said. "The last time there was a big flood two buildings near the river collapsed. Ed Dewey, the man who had the boat rental then, was almost killed."

I planted my feet more squarely on the floor, as if that would protect me if the shop fell apart.

"Rosa, I don't want to hurry you out," Madge said, "but I'm doing it. The weather's getting worse. You've had a long day, and more to come." When Rosa opened her mouth to protest, Madge added, "And you don't want to make Vejay stay out in this weather any later."

Rosa stood up. "My coat." She swallowed the last of her wine.

Madge handed her a heavy fisherman's jacket

and passed me my slicker. She hugged Rosa good-bye and avoided my gaze as she herded us out the door.

The truck was cold and the windows fogged almost as soon as we got in. I let the engine warm, then turned on the defroster.

"This is a nice truck, Vejay," Rosa said. The cold damp didn't seem to affect her. Growing up here, she would be used to it. I wondered if I would ever reach that state. "We used to have a defroster on Carlo's truck, but that went out five or six years ago and Carlo never got around to having it fixed. Of course, he was still fishing then. It was before the accident."

I shifted the truck into reverse and pulled out. The windshield wipers were on high, but there were still moments when I couldn't see through the rain.

"It was a storm like this, only it was April—salmon season," Rosa said. "Freak storm. Carlo was out fishing. In the ocean. The mast tore loose. It hit him, his hip. Broken."

The street was deserted, but the wind had snapped branches and thrown them onto the roadway. Leaving the truck in second gear, I drove, cautiously, in the middle of the road.

"The year after that he tried to fish, but with the rolling of the boats, he couldn't keep his balance. It was bad, very bad for him."

I turned right, up the sloping road to the house.

"I don't know why I'm carrying on like this, Vejay. You'll have to forgive me. I don't mean to cry on your shoulder. And there's really nothing to cry about. In the end it's just as well Carlo stopped fishing. There are so few fish anymore that it's all

Chris can do to make a living. Carlo's better off
doing repairs. With all the new people and the
bare hillsides around their new houses causing
slides, he's got more work than he can handle. The
river isn't like it was before either. There's rub-
bish, chemicals, who-knows-what's in it now. Not
fish anymore. The town's changing too. Plenty of
people resent it. But for Carlo it means work." She
looked over at me as I stopped the truck and
smiled. "Of course, there are people I'd rather not
admit that to."

"Like Ned Jacobs?"

She laughed. "You'll come in, Vejay?"

"Thanks, but no, Rosa. You had me over for
dinner last night and lunch today. I think it's
about time I visited my own house."

I watched her walk up the dark path to the
door. There was a light on inside. She waved,
turned, and the door opened. The light and
warmth seemed to wrap around her and pull her
into the safety of the house.

In the pickup I shivered. I was still in my PG&E
uniform, still wearing the slicker. I drove slowly
through town. The street was empty and the shops
closed.

I pondered over what I learned today. It seemed
like years since I'd left the substation, like another
lifetime. I recalled what Paul had said, and Patsy,
Skip, and Madge. And Sheriff Wescott. And still, I
came to the same conclusion. Frank was dealing
drugs. That was why he was meeting Patsy in the
state park. Either she was part of the delivery system, or merely a user. Either way, it explained
why she was so upset about Frank's murder.

I put the truck in the garage, pushed the garage

door shut behind me, and trudged up the fifty-two slippery steps to the house.

Once inside, I turned on the tub full blast, boiled a pot of water for the hot water bottle that would go between the sheets, and grabbed a book to read while I soaked.

The rain slashed against the windows. I thought I heard one of those trees I should have pruned scraping louder than usual against the side of the house. I started to undress, then remembered there were no logs drying inside for the morning's fire. I pulled my slicker back on and stepped out on the porch.

The rain hit my face; the branches crackled in the wind, but this was not loud enough to mask the sounds of a car or truck burning rubber on the street and a garage door slapping open in the rain.

I grabbed the flashlight that was lying next to my work gear inside the door and hurried, slipping, down the steps.

The garage door was flapping up and down. I pushed it up hard to the roof.

The truck was still there. I shone the light in the bed. Empty. But the hood had been pulled up. I pointed the light under it and stared.

The engine was a mess. It looked like someone had taken an axe to it.

CHAPTER 10

I called the Sheriff's Department, but at eleven at night, Wescott wasn't there, and I wasn't about to explain to someone new about Frank's death and how my engine was connected to it.

Logically, there was no reason to be afraid. The truck was a warning. Whoever did it wasn't going to come back now. That's why there are warnings.

But no amount of reason helped. What I wanted was to go to a motel, some place safe, and sign in under a false name. But, of course, I couldn't drive anywhere. I couldn't call one of my friends to come and get me, because one of my friends might not be a friend at all. I couldn't even bring myself to strip off my clothes and take the bath I'd yearned for all day.

Instead, I turned on every light in the house, hauled in the logs, spent an hour getting them to catch fire, and then sat there, still dressed, huddled in my quilt on the sofa all night.

Sometime during the night I fell asleep and didn't wake up until the phone rang at eight-thirty.

"Hello?" I said, still half asleep.

"Vejay Haskell?"

"Yes."

"Sheriff Wescott here."

It took me a moment to place him and longer to

realize why he was calling me. "My truck," I said, "it was attacked."

"Your truck was *attacked*?"

I described the condition of the engine. "The truck was in the garage. The garage door's been jimmied."

"There've been a lot of burglaries in your area lately. Ever since those Chinese brass plates were taken, it seems like the publicity encouraged all the regular housebreakers to think the whole Russian River area is an open field. And during any disaster, burglars assume the sheriff is tied up with mudslides and flood work and doesn't have time to check on houses."

"This was not a burglary. Nothing was stolen. And it's not vandalism either. No one breaks into a garage to damage an engine when there are trucks parked on the street.

"Are you sure the door was locked?"

"Yes. But that's beside the point. Look, I was talking to people all evening, asking about Frank. It'd be too much of a coincidence if the truck attack were not connected to that."

He said nothing.

I waited.

"Okay, don't touch the truck. I'll be out."

Before I could ask when, he hung up.

When turned out to be just long enough for me to take a shower, wash my hair, and make coffee. I had finished half the cup when the doorbell sounded.

Standing on my porch, the detective looked smaller than I remembered him, and somehow less threatening in the muted light of morning.

"It's not so bad," he said, stepping inside.

"What isn't?"

"I looked at your engine. Most of the damage is superficial. You won't be able to drive the truck now, but the engine itself looks unharmed. It's all mostly for show."

"Oh. Well, I guess that's a relief. I can call the auto club and have it towed into Guerneville, if the auto club is dealing with small stuff like this today."

"I'll have the department truck stop by. It's here in Henderson now. We've had some problem with a squad car."

"Thanks," I said, surprised.

"We are the servants of the citizens." He smiled; it was a smile born of confidence, the type of smile I like to see when discussing my truck.

"I just made some coffee. Do you want some?"

"Sure. I'm a sucker for decent coffee."

"Cream?"

"Real cream?"

"Well, no. Half-and-half. For here, that's cream."

"Okay, cream. No sugar."

When I returned with his mug, he was perched on the ottoman of my reading chair, the closest spot to the fire.

"Are you a heat lover?"

"I like novelty."

"You'll have to climb onto the logs if you want to get really warm."

"Don't you have heat?"

"I do, yes. It's just that . . ." I paused. He was waiting with an amused expectant expression. It was, I recalled, remarkably similar to Frank's. It was the look that had taken me in yesterday. "Meter readers have a few peculiarities. There's a lot of competitiveness among us, friendly rivalry."

"Such as?"

"Oh, how fast you can walk a route and still do it right. Doing it right is no issue. You make more than three mistakes per thousand, and you have explaining to do. But there are secret speed records for each route. And there's also low-key, ongoing bragging about how little electricity you can use. Since my house is all electric, I have to be very frugal with the heat if I want to have anything at all to say."

He laughed. Frank would have laughed. Frank would have felt that bit of foolishness deserved a drink on the house. Frank, now that I thought of that, was very generous when he chose to be. He had been more of a host than a bartender.

"I sit in my truck a lot in the winter."

He laughed again, but this time the laugh seemed less spontaneous. He pulled out a form from his briefcase. "We'll need a report. Tell me where you were with the truck last night."

I recounted the evening's visits with approximate times for each. "It was ten-thirty or quarter to eleven when I got home. It couldn't have been more than fifteen or twenty minutes before I heard the garage door banging."

"Did you notice another vehicle following you when you drove home?"

"No. But anyone who saw my truck in town could have guessed where I was headed."

"Did you see anything suspicious when you got to the garage? Were there any strange vehicles parked nearby?"

"I don't remember anything unusual. But it was late, and I was tired, and wet, and cold. All I wanted to do was get inside the house and take a bath. So I could have missed something."

Wescott put his pen down. "You said you spent last night talking to people about Frank Goulet. Just what was it you were asking them?" His face had hardened into that weathered look. Again I had the feeling he had replaced one facade with another, and there was no clue as to what existed beneath either.

I said, "I was asking them what they knew about Frank. Everyone is talking about Frank's death. And these people were Frank's friends."

"What did they tell you?"

"Nothing really."

"What exactly?"

"They told me what they would have told you if you had asked them. They said they didn't know anything about Frank being involved with drugs, but no one seemed surprised that the topic was broached."

"Is that all?"

It wasn't. I didn't mention Patsy's anger, or Skip's observation that there was something particular about the Place that attracted Frank, or Frank and Patsy meeting in the park, or Madge selling her shop. But these people were my friends. One might not be, but the others were. I didn't feel right telling the sheriff about them. And even if I did, what I knew was closer to gossip than fact. I said, "That's all."

"Detective work isn't as easy as it seems, is it?"

There was no need to reply to that. In the silence, he stood up and carried his cup to the

kitchen. And, irrationally, that show of fastidious-
ness annoyed me more.

"Do you have a sledgehammer, or an axe?" he
asked, stopping at the front door.

"No, why?"

"You have a pile of wood outside."

"I bought it."

"So you don't have an axe?"

"Are you suggesting that I wrecked my own engine?"

I had put the question lightly, I thought, but his
response was all business.

"I'm merely trying to find the weapon."

"Oh."

"The damage was superficial. Whoever did this
didn't intend to cause a lot of expense." He
walked out, closing the door.

I hesitated; I was tempted to follow him and
demand an explanation for his last statement. Just
because there weren't hundreds of dollars of damage, did he find this attack trivial? Did he assume
I'd done it myself? Did he consider it an attempt to
direct guilt elsewhere?

I left the door shut, walked back into the living
room, and sat down. With Wescott, I had no idea
what he thought. I didn't know whether he truly
suspected me, or didn't, or even if he understood
the threat made here.

I sat for about half an hour with my back to the
fire, feeling the cold on my chest. My house, which
had been a refuge from the cold and wet outside, a
place where I could be safe, now seemed isolated
and vulnerable. Whoever attacked my truck could
as easily have attacked me. The neighbors were
not alerted by the slapping of the garage door.

They would not have heard a muffled scream. Even with all the lights on, the house was too far up from the street, too "protected" behind tall trees, for anyone to look through the windows and see someone attacking me.

At best Wescott's reaction could be called non-committal. And even if he did believe me and decided to search elsewhere for Frank's killer, all I told him was that no one knew anything about Frank and drugs. That certainly wasn't going to prod him on. I really did need some solid evidence, something linking Frank to drugs. I wished now that I'd used those PG&E passkeys I'd been too angry to return, gone to Frank's Place last night and searched. There had to be some evidence there. If someone could break into my garage unnoticed, I could easily have let myself into Frank's Place with a key. I could have done it last night, when I still had a truck to drive there. Once inside the truck the rain and wind would have protected me, but to walk several miles through the rain, keeping off the street and out of sight when a flood was on its way, was out of the question. I'd had my chance and blown it.

I was still sitting in my chair when I heard a knock on the door. I jumped, before I realized that attackers rarely knock. And indeed, it was not an axe-wielding killer, but the driver of the sheriff's tow truck.

The driver of the tow truck left me at the garage. I was lucky, the mechanic told me. They could replace the air filter, put a sealant in the radiator, and do a couple of other things in the shop. I wouldn't have to go to a dealership in

Santa Rosa. That was good, he went on, since I'd
need to be towed and their truck had been gone all
day and probably would be just as busy next
week. My good fortune was even greater since
there was a lot of towing to be done now but not
much work for the mechanic. My truck would be
ready tomorrow.

My luck did not, however, include a ride back
to Henderson. That was five or six miles. If I
walked down North Bank Road in the daytime,
hitching a ride would be no problem. And as long
as I was in Guerneville, I called Ned Jacobs at the
state park, to convince him to come into town and
have lunch with me. No luck there either. Outsiders, Ned explained, had done a lot of damage to
the state park over the year. With the flood coming there was a lot of work to do. He couldn't take
a couple of hours off just because he wanted to.
And then, in a rush of remorse, he suggested dinner at six-thirty, when it would be too dark to
work. He'd come by.

I agreed. I liked Ned. I knew he liked me. As
long as Ned was kept off the topic of "outsiders,"
he could be fun. But alas, he was not going to
drive me home this afternoon.

I passed several restaurants, but somehow I
couldn't get up the ambition to go in. Eating a
meal seemed too formal, too time-consuming for
now, though I didn't know what I planned to do
with my time today anyway. I kept walking
through town to the Safeway store at the end. It
was the only supermarket around. With the exception of what I usually picked up at Thompson's, I
did most of my shopping here. As long as I was

going to be in the house that afternoon and the next day, I thought I might as well not starve.

Purposely, I took a small plastic basket, the kind you carry over your arm. I needed to show some self-control, in case I had to lug it all home by myself. Self-control, however, did not extend to chocolate, and I started with a large bar with peanuts, a favorite of meter readers in general. I made many mid-afternoon stops at Thompson's or its counterparts in other towns. Thompson's had actually increased their order last year on our account. In any case, I decided chocolate was not going to weigh down the grocery bag very much.

I added some greens, a couple of cans of soup, a dozen eggs, a package of cheese, a bottle of brandy to replace the one left at the Fernandezes', some tissues, and bread; just enough to disqualify me from the express check-out line. At slightly after twelve, the store was crowded, which surprised me. Then I realized this was pre-flood buying. The store was on low ground. On the wall by the check-cashing window was a photo of the flood of '64. Water covered the lower half of the picture window in front. I stepped out of line, added a few more cans, some coffee, and some Sterno for when the lights went out. The basket was heavy; the bag would be even heavier. I joined the end of the shortest line and picked up a tabloid off the rack by the check-out counter.

I had just finished reading the headlines, when I noticed Madge Oombs behind me.

CHAPTER

11

Apparently I was well-hidden behind the paper, because Madge Oombs was surprised and obviously not pleased to discover me. She took hold of her grocery cart and looked quickly at the next line, but while we had been standing there a few moments, three people had moved in behind her, and the other lines had grown longer too.

"Madge," I said, "I'm delighted to see you. Could you give me a lift home?" I watched her expression carefully, but the look of confusion, dismay, and resignation that greeted me told me nothing I didn't already know.

"Where's your truck?"

"In the shop. Engine trouble."

"Rotten time for that. It's a fairly new truck, isn't it?" The questions seemed straightforward. There was no hint of guilt or knowledge.

"I just bought it last year."

"Have you had problems with it before?"

The line moved forward. Two carts separated me from the check-out clerk.

"No, it's been fine."

"That's good. A reliable truck is important here."

I nodded. Glancing at the lines on either side of us, I spotted two women from town. If I recognized two people, there had to be five or six more whom Madge knew. Lowering my voice, I said, "Tell me about selling the shop, Madge."

She had followed my glances. Now she looked away.

"Madge," I said louder.

When she still didn't respond, I said, "I saw you and Skip at breakfast two days ago. I talked to Skip last night. I know about the two-year option clause. I know how valuable land right in town is, sewer or no sewer. And regardless how long it takes, the sewer is going to be completed sooner or later."

The line moved forward. A tall woman began to unload the first cart. She looked like she was buying enough to stock Thompson's. Beyond her, at the public phone, a man balanced a bag in one arm as he flipped through the yellow pages.

"Madge," I lied, "the reason I know for sure that you're selling is that I called the phone company."

"The phone company?" She looked at me as if I'd lost my mind.

"The business office. I gave them your name. I asked if they had all the information for your next year's listing. They said they had no listing at all for the shop next year."

She shrugged. "I haven't gotten around to it."

"That's not what they said." I hoped I wouldn't have to go any further with this; I was straining my imagination. "You're cancelling."

"Vejay . . ."

"Who are you selling to?"

She looked quickly to either side and in a whisper, said, "Oh, okay. I've given a lease option on the property to a developer."

"For a shopping complex?"

"Condominiums."

I nodded.

She rolled the cart forward, then pulled it back. "Look, I've lived here all my life. I've worked at that shop for twenty years. It does reasonably well for what it is, but I don't make any fortune." Her voice was still a whisper, her face taut. "My life hasn't been easy. I've had two husbands. One died and the other tried to drink himself to death. They left me with nothing. I'm tired of scraping by."

"But you don't want people to know, right?"

"It's part of the deal. I agreed to say nothing until he completes a couple of other deals."

The line moved again. The woman ahead of me began to unload her groceries.

"Options on the shops on either side of yours?"

She nodded reluctantly.

I wondered how much Madge's silence was costing her neighbors.

"I'm not a fanatic about this town like some of you new people. I don't sit on my deck and sip Chablis and fuss because sensible people want a sewer line. I just want to be able to live decently."

"How much will you get when the option is exercised?"

She didn't answer.

"Madge," I said louder.

"Market price and a percentage of the condos," she hissed.

"Did Frank know about this?"

She glanced around again, evaluating the line to our right. She nodded at an elderly man toward the rear. Turning back to me, she looked less flustered than before. "Frank?" she said. "Why would

I tell him? I've only talked to Frank the few times he was in my shop, and that's been twice in the last year. I already told you about that."

"Tell me again."

"I told you, he was asking how I ran the store. He wanted to know where I got the things I sold—did I buy them locally, did I go to auctions or follow up ads in the paper? Did I deal primarily in glass or metal, or was there any plan at all? All he needed to do was look around if he wanted to know what I sold. I told him that. I don't have time for idle chatter." Madge stopped talking, with obvious relief.

The woman in front of me had moved up. I lifted my basket to the counter, removed the groceries, put a ten-dollar bill on the counter, and turned back to Madge. "What else did he want to know?"

"I don't recall, Vejay. It was a long time ago. I can't remember his questions."

"Well, what did you tell him?"

The clerk handed me my change. I stepped forward, giving Madge room to get to the counter. Her own cart was next to the register and the clerk was tallying her groceries.

"Madge?"

"I told him about various people who opened antique shops and failed. It looks, to an outsider, like you do nothing but sit behind the cash register and take in money, but you do have to know something. People are not going to pay the same price for redwood as they would for mahogany. You have to recognize which mirrors can be salvaged. You need to know how to care for leathers and bronzes. Brasses you can let sit forever, but bronzes you need to keep free from humidity. There's a tale of an antique dealer who bought an expensive bronze buddha in Japan and had it shipped back here. He didn't know what he was doing. He had the buddha crated but he didn't seal it in a humidity-controlled package." She took two twenties from her purse and handed them to the checker.

I waited, blocking her exit.

The checker put her bags in the cart and Madge took it. But if I'd worried about Madge escaping, the fear was needless. She continued, "So the ship left the cold of Japan and hit a hot spell, and then the weather changed back and became cold again. Condensation formed on the bronze exterior of the buddha. The moisture was held in by the wrapping. By the time it was uncrated, the finish was ruined." She loaded the bags into the cab of her truck, opened the driver's door, and climbed in. Without giving me a glance, she backed out of the parking lot.

It might have been more sensible to wait till I'd gotten my ride home before asking unwanted questions. But, of course, in the privacy of her own truck Madge wouldn't have admitted anything.

Burdened with my groceries, I walked through the lot and around to the main road. It was an odd story, the one about the buddha. Had Frank found it odd? Had Madge thrust it on him to get rid of him as she had done with me? Was it a true story, or did she create the whole thing to kill time until she could shake me off?

And more to the point, what did Frank know or
suspect about her selling the shop? It was clear she
wanted, and needed, secrecy. Had Frank been a
danger to that?

I managed to hitch a ride home, but not before I walked through a few puddles and was splashed by several cars. When I got home I settled into a warm bath. My life these days seemed to be spent continually in water. Only the temperature changed.

I contemplated everything Madge told me, but it was not fitting in like the missing pieces of a puzzle. Why did Frank ask her about her business? I couldn't believe, as she did, that he was planning to branch out into antiques. There would have been no reason for that. As Madge said, the business didn't bring a great income, and it did require a lot of time. Frank needed all his time for the Place. So what was he after? Was he interested in knowing who came regularly to Henderson; who might buy and sell things besides antiques? And that led back to the question of drugs and the fact that I had no proof. It became clearer and clearer that I was accomplishing nothing but alienating people with my probing and I would continue doing so until I had definite evidence about the drugs. I was having dinner with the only friend I hadn't yet put off, and by the end of the evening he probably would join the list of the offended. I heartily wished that I had checked out Frank's

Place the previous night when I still had the pickup. This evening I was going nowhere.

I heard brakes squeal in the driveway just before six. Ned Jacobs was a notoriously rotten driver. Perhaps it was all that unsupervised time in the state park. Perhaps it was the monotony of the job and the long distances along dirt roads he had to cover. Whatever, Ned had virtually no familiarity with the first three gears; anything under fourth was merely a fleeting stage. At every start, he would challenge the zero-to-sixty record. It was fortunate Ned had a professional relationship with the sheriff's department, or he would have spent most of his time in residence at the jail.

Now he jogged up the steps with mountain-goat surety and banged on the door.

"Not formal, okay?" he said. He was in jeans and a wool shirt.

I was in jeans and a wool sweater. "So you're not taking me to the Top of the Mark?"

"I thought we'd go to Jenner and see what the ocean's up to."

"Is the road clear to the beach?"

"So they say. My truck'll make it."

We clambered down the steps—he easily in his ranger's boots, me clinging to the rail—and into the truck. I was sure his faith in it was justified. It was a big Chevy four-wheel drive that made my little pickup look like something a toddler would be straddling. As he stepped on the gas, spraying mud in all directions, metal things in the truck bed jumped and clanked. He skidded to a stop at the light three blocks away.

From there the journey was an act of faith. We passed under the canopy of trees I loved in the

link of an eye. The empty shops and houses
long the river were mere sodden blurs. On the
adio the announcer reported the high-water levels
ll the way up the river; he listed the increasing
umber of slide areas and the evacuation centers
eadying for the flood. Some of those centers, I'd
eard, held annual gatherings which served the
ame families year after year. For them evacua-
ions had become events in themselves, and as
oon as the water reached thirty feet upriver,
nothers began cooking their specialties, fathers
arried camping gear to the centers, and children
athered balls and games and transistor radios.

Jenner was half an hour along the river from
Henderson. Here the river emptied into the Pa-
ific, and the town, clinging with surprising tenac-
y to the hillside, overlooked the ocean. The Jen-
er Point Restaurant was at the top of the hill on a
ocky cliff. If you sat by the front window you saw
nothing below but the spray of breakers. We made
he trip in twenty minutes, and since most sensible
people were home filling sandbags or boarding
vindows, we had our choice of tables.

"I'm starved," I said. "So far today I've had a
andy bar."

"Wine?" Ned asked. "Is that okay on an empty
tomach?"

"Fine. My stomach won't be empty long."

We ordered and I started on the French bread.
Ned talked about the park, the trees that had al-
eady fallen, the creeks that were poised to over-
low, the underbrush that was creating unwanted
lams. "It's a mess. No matter what I do, it's a
ness."

"Maybe you should just wait."

"Can't."

I shrugged and ate the last piece of bread.

"It's awful about Frank," he said.

"You two were good friends, weren't you?" had, of course, planned to bring up the subjec and was relieved when he mentioned it first.

He hesitated. "I saw him a lot."

"But?"

"Well, it's probably nothing. It's just that the first time I saw Frank he'd been in a fight with a camper. It was over a woman. Frank got the decidedly short end of it. I patched him up quite a bit before he could go home. He didn't say much, but the next year, a whole year later, the camper reported his tires slashed and a lot of his gear destroyed."

"And you think Frank did that?" I asked, amazed.

"I'm almost positive. I saw him in the park the night it happened."

"Still, why would he wait a whole year if he was looking for revenge?"

"I don't know. I'm not defending his actions. I'm just telling you about the incident. I saw Frank plenty of other times, and he seemed pleasant, normal—just Frank. Everyone likes the park. And I enjoyed a few beers at Frank's Place. We had some common interests, like preserving the area. He talked about that a lot."

I could imagine. Ned talked about keeping the area unchanged to anyone who would listen. "Outsiders" were to Ned what finances were to Paul Fernandez. With Ned, Frank would have had difficulty avoiding the topic.

Still, I said, "I never heard Frank mention the population changes here."

"Really? He was adamant about not wanting the town to grow or change."

Dinner arrived—fresh salmon, a baked potato smothered in sour cream, and a heap of asparagus. I took a bite, a couple of bites, while I formulated a tactful question. "It would seem like expansion would have been good for Frank's business."

"He didn't need more trade. He had plenty."

"Did he say that?"

"He didn't have to."

"It's odd, though, that he never mentioned so strong a conviction—I mean, to anyone but you." I took a forkful of asparagus, watching him from under my eyelashes as I lifted the spears to my mouth.

But Ned apparently saw nothing pointed in my question. "Frank," he said, "was a merchant. He had to appear impartial on controversial issues unless he wanted to lose trade. So he only talked freely to individual friends. He even asked me not to mention his feelings. I had some questions about that, I certainly wouldn't be able to keep my feelings hidden. But then I hardly need to attract more people to the park."

"But how do you know Frank didn't tell someone else something entirely different and swear *them* to secrecy?"

Ned stared at me. "Frank wouldn't do that."

"Why not? Merchants do make use of people."

"He wouldn't have made use of *me*. I would have realized."

"Well, he was murdered, so there was someone he either made use of or wasn't straight with."

"It wasn't me. Do you think I've been in the woods too long, that I only deal with chipmunks and bunny rabbits? I've got enough sense to know if a friend is lying to me." He grabbed his glass and took a big swallow of wine. "Besides, what would Frank have gained? He came to see me maybe once a week. That's a lot of time to spend talking about something you've no interest in." He picked up his fork and stuck it into his salmon. I had never really looked at his hands; they were big, thick, the result of years of manual work.

Ned was one of those men who always seemed smaller than he actually was. His clothes were always baggy, and he looked thin. His dark hair had just enough wave to make it look unruly, but not enough curl to give it imposing bulk. His features were small, sharp, his eyes a pale green, and now, in March, his skin was very pale. Had he been a poet, freezing in a New York garret (circa 1920), he would have looked the part. But he was strong; he had the endurance to spend entire days slogging through the park, lifting debris, cutting branches. Yet every time I realized how substantial a man he was, I was newly surprised.

"I hadn't realized Frank came to see you that often," I said.

"Well, he didn't always stay." Ned looked abashed. "Sometimes he was just walking in the park and I ran into him. Sometimes he stopped in."

Things were getting a little clearer. "Did you ever see him with Patsy?"

"Of course."

"In the park?"

"Well . . ."

"Well?"

"Yes, but not always."

"But often?"

"Pretty often. Maybe once or twice a month. But, Vejay, I don't think there was anything between them. Lots of people walk in the park. Lots of people run into each other."

"Of course," I said, not believing a word of it. If Frank had used the park as a rendezvous with Patsy, it explained why he needed to stay on Ned's good side. And if Frank had so easily fooled Ned, I wondered how facilely he'd handled the rest of us. Was the Frank I had known anything like the real Frank?

We ordered dessert and listened to the waves slam against the cliffs outside. Then we made our way back to his truck and wound down a back route he found through the town.

"I love discovering new streets, seeing the ocean from a different vista. I even love the river when it floods," he said, on one of the few straight stretches of road.

"It's still a vacation, isn't it?"

"Yeah, I guess so. I guess I'm still the kid I used to be when I came up here in the summers." He slammed on the brakes at the bottom of the hill. "Even now, it's not the same. It's so much more commercial, the whole area. All those new spiffy motels, instead of the seedy old cabins with the white paint half peeled off."

"Charming."

"What?"

"That's what they call them in real estate lingo."

He laughed. "I know they leave a lot to be de-

sired. I wouldn't be crazy about staying in one.
But they were once part of the area."

"Part of your childhood?"

"Yes."

He was driving slower now, though still not at
the speed limit. A few miles outside town, he
slipped an arm around my shoulder with the same
awkwardness I recalled in high school boys.

"You weren't real involved with Frank, were
you?" he asked in such a wary tone that it was
apparent that this was the question the evening
had been leading up to.

"No, not at all. Why did you think that?"

"Rumor. I don't know. Frank was good with
women. He was, well, Frank. Chris could tell you
stories from when they were on ship together. He
said he always got second choice, if there was a
second choice left."

"Frank certainly has got the reputation of going
through women like fruit on a Safeway counter."

"I didn't mean—"

"No. I'm just getting tired of hearing that question. I suppose we're both tired. You've had a hard
day and tomorrow won't be any easier." I liked
Ned, but I saw him as a friend, and I didn't want
to deal with anything more. Not now.

If Ned caught my hint, he chose to ignore it. His
arm still rested self-consciously on my shoulder.
Instead he responded to my comment. "It's always
busy in the park. They need more staff. Tomorrow
will be worse in some ways, but at least there
won't be people there. There are too many roads,
too many entrances. I check the ones that I can,
but there's no way we can make sure all the gates
are closed—all the people are out at night."

"But that must just be in the summer."

"You'd think. In the summer it's party time, people strewing paper plates and beer cans, lighting fires. In the winter, who knows? Anything could be going on there. If I were a spy, it would be the number-one spot to pass my messages."

"Or to deal drugs?"

He laughed. "That goes without saying. I'm just pleased when it's something that doesn't have to be lit." He slammed to a stop at the Henderson traffic light. Whatever awkwardness he might have in positioning his right arm, he made up for with his left. He held the steering wheel rock steady.

It was dark, and, of course, pouring, as he pulled into my driveway. Goodbyes, I decided, were to be made in the truck. As I turned to him to say my thanks, he tightened his grip and drew me forward. His kiss was surprisingly soft, unexpectedly pleasant.

It wasn't until I got out that I noticed the axe in the back of the truck.

It was perfectly reasonable for Ned Jacobs to have an axe in his truck. It would have been unthinkable for a ranger not to. Had he been the one who smashed my truck engine, he would surely have thought to put his axe out of sight. I told myself all that as I climbed up the stairs, ran the bath water, and turned it off to let it drain out instead. I told myself that I suspected everyone, that I saw killers surrounding me, harrassment from the sheriff, and menace from my friends. Again I wished that I had my pickup, that I could breeze down to Frank's Place, turn that PG&E key

I still had in my pocket, flick on my reliable PG&E flashlight, and find a handful of telltale marijuana leaves.

Now, not only did I not have transportation to get there, but Ned and Madge (and therefore Rosa and everyone she had talked to) knew that I had no way to leave the house. Whoever attacked my truck certainly knew.

I stood shivering over the draining tub. Then I pulled my down vest out of the closet, retrieved my PG&E rain gear from the hook by the door, took out the route keys and my own keys, and piled them all on the chair near the door. Perhaps everyone's knowing I couldn't make it over to Frank's Place tonight would work to my advantage.

It was 10:15, still too early to leave the house without being seen. But there was one other thing I needed to do before I left.

I dialed the Fortimiglio number. Chris answered.

"Hi, Chris, this is Vejay Haskell."

"Hi, Vejay."

"How're things at your house?"

"Okay. Dad's at my sister Frannie's in Guerneville helping her get ready for the flood. Her husband works nights now."

"Isn't he fishing with you?"

"No. He used to. But there aren't enough fish to support us all. So Ralph got this job in Santa Rosa. If the fishing gets better he'll come back."

"Maybe for salmon season," I said.

"Maybe. But the salmon hasn't been doing well either. There's getting to be too much pollution in the river. Too many businesses and people pouring stuff in."

"Well, maybe when the sewer is finished, it'll be better."

"I doubt it," he said. "Mom's here. Do you want to talk to her? She's making pasta and bottling sauce so we won't starve if the power goes out."

"You'll be better prepared than I am."

"We've been through floods before, and there's always room for one more here, Vejay."

"Thanks. Listen, it's you I called to talk to. I have to ask you a rather peculiar question."

"Uh-huh?"

"If you wanted to bring say fifty pounds of bulky stuff off a ship and up the river, how would you do it?"

Chris laughed.

It was not the response I expected.

"Chris?"

"Well, Vejay, you wouldn't. You couldn't bring anything upriver. They have to dredge the outlet every year so the salmon can get through. So if you're planning on moving something bigger than a salmon, you'd better get a truck."

"No way at all?"

"None that I know. Surely you've been to Jenner and seen the beach."

"Yes, as a matter of fact I was there tonight. I guess I just wasn't thinking."

"What are you bringing in? Are you considering smuggling?" He laughed again.

"Nothing so exciting. A friend offered me a couple of heavy blankets and some nice quilts and two bean bag chairs, if I could get them from his boat when he comes down the coast. But now I think it would be more trouble than it's worth."

"Does your friend fish around here?" Chris, in Fortimiglio fashion, longed for every detail.

I felt bad about lying to him, and worse about the prospect of this story getting out of hand. "No, Chris. He has a pleasure craft. He's from Oregon," I added for good measure.

"Oh."

"Well, thanks Chris," I said quickly. "Say hello to your parents for me."

"Sure thing."

"Bye."

I hung up the phone. It was still too early to go to Frank's. The walk would take an hour, maybe more. Once I got over the bridge onto South Bank Road, I would be safe. It was while going through town and crossing the bridge that I might be spotted. I had to wait until the roads were empty.

I pictured the walk along the three blocks into town, through this end of town, past Thompson's, across the bridge, then right on South Bank Road, along the mushy side of the road, past closed-up motels, cabins, and two restaurants that opened only for the summer trade. I'd pass along a ridge that led down to the beach, past Paul and Patsy's canoe rental, past more houses, more motels. It would be a long, wet walk. No one would suspect me of going there on foot because no sane person would try it.

The more I thought about it, the colder, wetter, and longer the trip seemed. Did I really need to know what was at Frank's Place? Couldn't I leave the investigation to the sheriff?

But the sheriff was investigating *me*. Someone was threatening me. And I was suspicious of every one of my friends. If I didn't find evidence to show the sheriff, nothing would change—at least not for the better.

I had to go. But there was another way of getting there, although it meant waiting until later. Lacking a preferable plan for the next hour and a half, I reran the water in the tub. This time I climbed in.

It was after midnight when I left the house. Outside it was totally dark—no streetlights, headlights, or taillights—and the rain clouds blocked the slightest suggestion of a moon. The rain splattered loudly against my slicker; it blocked out the sounds of the night. As I carefully stepped down the stairs I heard nothing but the noise of my own feet and the rain.

The street was empty. Still, I wished my slicker were brown or navy instead of bright yellow.

I cut north the block before town, skirting the shops. There was no one in sight here either. No streetlights. Even the interior lights of the houses were off. Half-running, I covered the two blocks to the substation.

I glanced behind me, and ahead, and behind me again. Nothing moved. I hesitated. I was still safe. I could go home to bed and still be a law-abiding citizen. I still had a choice.

I looked around again, but no one came to save me.

Taking a breath, I pulled out my employee key, opened the gate, and walked through—a burglar. Silently I pushed the gate shut, listened, and, hearing nothing, ran across the lot to the office.

The back door light shone bright even in the rain. It made it possible for any passing car to see my outline. I looked behind, but nothing was visible. Fumbling, I found the door key on my ring, got it in the lock on the second try, and opened the door.

No alarm sounded. Beside the door was the pegboard with the truck keys. I grabbed the ring for number twelve, the newest and most reliable truck, and caught myself before reaching for the sign-out sheet to initial out the truck as I did each working day.

Pulling the door shut behind me, I stepped out of the light and checked the street. Still no sign of movement. I ran across the lot to the trucks, squatting behind each one to read its number until I came to twelve. I stuck the key in the lock. I could still turn back. I still hadn't done much. I could return the key and go home and no one would know. I could . . .

I climbed into the truck, listened again for the sound of a car. I wished I knew how often the sheriff patrolled the area.

Hearing nothing, I backed the truck into the center of the lot, pulled up to the gate, got out and opened it, drove the truck through, and then walked back to lock it. Only then did I turn on the headlights.

I headed left toward the ocean, staying on the back street till I got through town, then cut down to North Bank Road. I'd go by the long route and cross the west bridge, avoiding the town altogether. It was the route I'd taken back from Frank's the day he'd been killed.

The road was empty. The rain fell heavily but did not blur the windshield. Once or twice I passed a house with a lamp on, but mostly the road was dark. It wasn't until I turned onto the bridge that I saw headlights in the other lane. I pressed hard on the gas pedal, then reminded myself to force myself to ease off, to drive at a normal speed and not draw attention to myself. I passed the car and caught the image of an older sedan—definitely not a patrol car—in my peripheral vision. Still, my stomach was jumping.

I turned left on South Bank Road, back toward Frank's. Here, somehow it seemed less deserted. Even though they were closed, boarded, and sand-bagged, motels and cabins stood along the road. There could be people lurking behind them. But surely, no one, not even the horniest teenager, would be parked beside a low-lying motel right before the flood.

I slowed as I passed Frank's. Would the sheriff have a guard there? I hadn't considered that. There was no patrol car in the parking area, no one visible standing outside the door. I couldn't see into the lot behind the building. It might hold twenty sheriffs, but there was no way to check. I drove on.

Two hundred yards past Frank's, I pulled the truck into an alley across the street and parked behind a deserted motel. I wished there was a util-ity pole there, something to give the truck the sug-gestion of legitimacy. But then even that would not be really safe. I was driving a meter reader's pickup, not a repair truck.

I climbed down, locked the door, and made my way back to the street. Through the rain I could hear the strong waters of the river rushing along thirty yards ahead. I ran across South Bank Road, past the house on the river side and into its back yard. It, I hoped, was one of the unoccupied ones. I'd been past here a hundred times, and I couldn't recall whether it was vacant or not.

I hurried across the yard, behind the motel next door, on the mushy grass ridge that dropped fif-teen feet down to the river in the summer. Now the river lapped at its edge. River spray hit my raincoat. Something heavy in the water smashed against the bank. I froze, waited, looked around, then moved forward.

On the far side of the motel was Frank's parking lot. It looked empty. I stepped out from the shelter of the motel. Headlights turned into the lot. I stared, then forced myself to move back against the motel wall.

The lights moved forward, then stopped. I held my breath, waiting for the driver to get out. The car didn't move. I stood stone still. And then the lights pulled back. It was probably just turning around. I couldn't make out the type of the car, or if it bore an insignia. But surely a sheriff would check me out if he'd seen me.

But a civilian wouldn't. He'd go home and call the sheriff. Had he seen me? Had I gotten back against the building in time? There was no way to know. And now, the thought of going back to the truck, driving it to the substation, and going home, seemed worse than running across the lot to Frank's Place.

I pulled out my keys and squinted to find Frank's. Taking a breath, I ran at full speed across the lot to the back door, thrust the key in the lock, and pushed the door open.

The door led into an alcove next to the bar. I'd been in here before, of course, to read the meter. Usually there were several coats and assorted rain gear hanging from hooks, and miscellaneous cans stacked against the wall. I shone the flashlight on the meter. It was as I'd seen it a few days ago. The rain gear was gone, but cans of juice—grape, apricot, and pineapple—blocked the bottom two feet of the wall. Otherwise, the tiny room was empty.

I stepped into the bar itself. My eyes grew ac-

customed to the dark. I could make out the bar,
the stools, and beyond the tables and chairs to the
front windows. In its emptiness, the room seemed
much smaller than it had when it was filled with
people eating and drinking, with Rosa rushing
through carrying another bottle of spaghetti sauce,
with Frank laughing at the bar. I shook off the
uneasy feeling. No time for nostalgia. No sense in
bothering with the tables. Nothing would be hidden out there.

I stopped behind the bar and flashed the light
under it, at open shelves of glasses. An icemaker,
unplugged now, held water. On the wall behind
the bar were the bottles; the ones on top were
open, the others waited in readiness, but there
were no cupboards, no containers that did not
open. Everything here was what it seemed to be.

The bathroom was at the other side of a small
hallway. It reminded me of a camping facility—
tiny, dank, with a toilet, a sink, and peeling paint.

Crammed in at the end of the hallway, between
the bathroom and bar, was a two-foot high metal
cabinet. The sliding door was locked, but I had
seen Frank take its key off a hook from around the
corner in the bar. I had seen him and I suspected
many other customers had, so it was unlikely that
anything Frank wanted to keep hidden would be
in this cabinet.

I unlocked it and slid the door to one side, shin-
ing the light on the upper shelf. Papers lay on it
haphazardly—orders for liquor, for mixers, payment receipts for laundry. There must have been
thirty various sheets. I gathered them into a pile
and dropped them in a plastic bag in my pocket.
In the corner was a ledger checkbook. Deciding it

was too risky to take that, I noted the balance—
$2694.75—and left it in the cabinet.

The bottom shelf was empty. I relocked the cabinet and returned the key to its hook in the bar.

I hadn't really expected to find anything in the bar, the bathroom, the cabinet, or anywhere else inside. In its entirety, Frank's Place consisted of the bar and the small restaurant beyond. To the left of the bar was the alcove that led to both the customers' door and the back door I'd come in tonight. To the right was the hall and the bathroom. The trap door had to be in the hall. And it was through the trap door that I *did* expect to find the evidence of Frank's involvement in drug dealing.

I flashed my light on the indoor-outdoor carpet, then bent down, lifted up an end and rolled it back until it cleared the trap door. Catching the ring at one side, I pulled. Nothing happened. I pulled again. It jerked but held. I pulled a third time, glad for my meter-reader muscles, and the door lifted free.

Beneath it was darkness. The water in the inlet splashed against the building. In the river beyond, frenzied currents smashed branches against the shore. After the silence in the bar, this sounded like breakers pounding the cliffs in Jenner.

Placing the flashlight beside me, I knelt and stuck my head through the opening. Spray hit my eyes. I shook my head, opened my eyes again, and stared down. The water appeared to be six feet beneath the door. There was, or had been, a hole dug at this end of the inlet directly beneath the trap door so the illegal liquor could be lowered and hidden. The hole would be, I imagined, about the size of those abandoned cesspools I kept stumbling into. Was it still there now? Could something as dry and bulky as marijuana be kept there? If so, how? I looked around. There were no ropes, nothing connecting the hole if it existed, to the trap door. I beamed the flashlight down, but it showed only water slapping against the building.

Pushing myself up, I turned off the flashlight and walked back through the bar to the entry hall, grabbed the largest can of apricot juice, and hurried back to the trap door. Beaming the light down, I dropped the can. Even through the splashing water, I had hoped to hear a telltale clunk to give me an idea how far down the hole went. But there was no clunk. Either the hole was covered in soft mud, or it was too deep for the sound to be heard.

I leaned farther through the trap door, hanging on with one arm. I flashed the light in a circle under the building. There was soggy land on one side, water on another, and the building on the two remaining sides. Aiming the light up around the bottom of the door told me nothing more. It was the wooden bottom of the Place, with nothing hanging, no nooks or other doorways. Nothing was hidden; there was no place to hide anything.

Disgusted, I pushed myself back up and sat against the wall. I had been so sure that the secret place would be connected to the trap door. Suddenly, I was exhausted. I felt I should search through the restaurant once more, on general principle, but I couldn't get up the energy to move. I certainly didn't want to go back outside. Now that I was in here it seemed so safe, so overwhelmingly difficult to just get up and leave.

So I sat and stared at the wall, trying to remember what had convinced me there would be a hiding place here. I had decided that Frank was dealing drugs. The drugs had to be kept somewhere. Frank specifically wanted the Place. If he came to Henderson for a purpose, then he bought the Place with that purpose in mind. Therefore the drugs were being sold through the Place. They had to be here somewhere.

I slumped farther down the wall. There was something else, some other reason I had questions about the Place. Before I thought of the drugs. The drugs had been the outgrowth . . .

Of course! The overread! Whatever Frank was doing here, it was using a lot of electricity. I got up, flashed the light around the hallway. There were no wires visible. Likewise, the bathroom only held what it should.

In the bar, I moved much more slowly, peering behind the glasses, following the beam of the flashlight, looking for any unexplained wire. The only connections here were to the ice maker, the refrigerator, and the small stove used to heat Rosa's dinners.

The far wall, with the bottles lined along it, took longer. I had to move each one, then put it back. Twice the river smashed debris against the building supports. Twice I jumped, froze, waited, then moved carefully back to the wall. It wasn't until I reached the end near the alcove where I'd entered that I spotted the cord leading down behind the gallon wine jugs, around the corner, to the alcove.

It led nowhere. The plug had been tossed into the corner. There was nowhere for it to go. Noth-

ing in the alcove was electric, save for the bulb on
the ceiling. There was no reason to have an exten-
sion cord here, unless it led to something not
readily visible.

And that explained the high, precarious pile of
juice cans. I shoved them away from the wall, bar-
ing a two-and-a-half foot square door.

I pulled it open and flashed the light inside. The
space was about twelve feet long and two-and-a-
half feet high. Its floor was level with the alcove,
so it would not be spotted from the outside. As I
looked at it I realized that it was cut into the wall
behind the bar. It was not totally hidden from
anyone who looked for it, but it was hardly visible
to the casual observer. I flashed the light toward
the back and sighed.

It was empty except for two space heaters and a
dehumidifier. They certainly explained the dis-
crepancy in Frank's bill. And why he didn't want
me to check into it.

I looked carefully at the floor. If marijuana had
been stored here, surely there would be a leaf, a
stem. But I could see nothing. I crawled in. Even
close up there was no sign of anything more exotic
than dust. I moved to the far end. For the first time
since I'd come inside Frank's Place I was scared.
The room was sepulchral—no windows, of
course, not even a crack for light or air to come
through. It smelled tomblike.

I ran a finger along the floor, feeling for shreds
of leaf or crushed seeds. But there were none. My
finger moved smoothly, unhindered. I stopped.
This wasn't a normal wood floor like the one in
the bar. It was too smooth. I flashed the light
closer. I looked at the walls, the corners. The

whole room had been varnished with poly-
urethane. No wonder it smelled tomblike. No
wonder no air moved. The room had been completely sealed.

If the small door completed the seal, and there
was no reason to think it wouldn't, the room
would be virtually airtight. It was a tomb.

Forcing myself to remain calm, I shone the light
inch by inch along the floor. But there was nothing
there—no leaves, no stems, not one seed. I was
about to turn off the flashlight when I spotted a
wadded sheet of newspaper in a recessed corner by
the door. It looked like it had been used to wrap
something. Carefully, so as to preserve anything
that might be inside, I picked it up and put it in a
plastic bag in my pocket.

I flashed the light back to the corner. Under
where the paper had been, was a tarnished metal
plate, the size of an ashtray. Perhaps this was what
Frank had used to separate the marijuana leaves
and seed from the stems. Perhaps there would still
be a remnant of leaf clinging to it. I stuck it in my
last plastic bag, put it in my other pocket, and
snapped the pocket shut.

I gave the room one more cursory check. With
relief I crawled halfway out the door.

Footsteps sounded on the stairs outside.

I stopped. The headlights in the parking lot! The
driver of the car must have called the sheriff!
Should I back up and pull the door shut behind
me? Entomb myself?

But cans were spread over the alcove.

Metal scraped in the door lock.

I crawled forward into the alcove. The front
door was opposite. I pushed, but it was locked.

My key was to the back door only, the one with
someone on the other side.

Where to hide? I ran behind the bar.

I could hear the door handle turn.

There was nowhere to hide. There was only one
thing to do.

I ran to the trap door and jumped into the water.

CHAPTER
14

The hole under the trap door was deep. The water covered my head.

I clambered up, scrambling for footholds on one side, pushing against the dead weight of my rain gear. I slipped again, down under, and came up gasping. With a lunge, I grabbed a support beam and pulled myself out of the hole and into the inlet. A branch banged against my arm and chest, pushing me back, but I hung on and hoisted myself up onto the bank.

Only then did I think of the person inside Frank's Place. But I didn't stop to look back at the trap door as I clambered up the bank. I ran, sloshing in my water-filled boots, until I was safe behind the motel.

I listened, expecting to hear footsteps, to see a flashlight beam. I bent one knee back, letting the water drain from the boot. I waited, listening, then drained the other boot. But there were no menacing sounds.

There was no vehicle in the parking lot, but that meant nothing. My truck wasn't in the lot either.

I shivered violently. Everything I had on was wet and icy cold. If I didn't leave now, whoever was in Frank's Place would be able to trail me by the clatter of my teeth.

I made my way back over the empty yard and

across the street to the truck. Silently I thanked the
powers at PG&E for snap-shut pockets and fished
out the keys that snuggled safely on my right side.
Climbing in, I turned on the engine and the windshield wipers.

Very briefly I considered driving past Frank's
Place with the lights off, in hopes of seeing a vehicle in the far lot and finding out whether it belonged to the sheriff. But common sense coupled
with fear told me that I would be much more visible to him than he would be to me.

I turned right, driving in first gear with the
lights off till I was a couple hundred yards down
the road, listening all the while for engine sounds
which I probably wouldn't even be able to hear
over the wind and rain.

The drive back to the PG&E lot seemed like one
big block of time. It was the middle of the night
and I saw no other vehicles, no pedestrians. The
lights at either end of the bridge blinked amber
and I didn't even pause. It was only when I
reached North Bank Road that I stopped to consider, then quickly reject, the idea of going home
and changing into dry clothes before returning the
truck.

The PG&E lot was still empty. I parked the
truck, replaced the keys, and walked the icy blocks
home without seeing a soul.

It wasn't till I got back in my own house that
the full terror hit me. I felt neither safe nor relieved. And it was twenty minutes before I could
think clearly enough to consider the results of my
investigations—specifically, what I had in the
plastic bags in my pockets. Even then my hands
were shaking too much to deal with the snaps.

I took off the slicker, rolled up my sleeves, put both wrists under the tap, and held them there until I felt warmth up and down my arms. The shaking in my hands subsided. Then I opened the pocket snaps on the slicker and pulled out the three plastic bags.

The first one contained a metal dish, the size of an ashtray. It was once yellow metal but was pretty thoroughly oxidized now. In the center I could make out some indentations or decoration, but the tarnish muddied any clear design. And, more to the point, holding the dish up near the light, I could spot no remnant of marijuana leaf, stem, or seed. I had a magnifying glass in the living room. Taking the dish and the two remaining plastic bags up there I held it in front of a lamp. Still no telltale trace showed. Maybe the sheriff's lab could find something, but that wouldn't help me.

Disgusted, I stuck the dish on the mantel next to a pile of catalogs I had planned to burn.

I pulled the white sheet off my bed and spread it on the living room floor. Carefully, I extracted the wadded newspaper from the plastic bag and straightened it out over the sheet. The only telltale evidence that landed on the sheet was a plastic knob, the type that could be found on a lamp or a radio. Probably a twenty-cent item. No leaf, no stem, etc.

The paper itself was the front page from the *San Francisco Chronicle,* dated January 15. The headline article read ECONOMIC SLUMP DEEPENS. The other front page stories discussed San Francisco politics, a scandal in the housing authority, another shipping line's move to the Port of Oakland, and over-

crowding at the SPCA. The back page was given
entirely to continuations of the front page articles.
I turned the sheet over to 2 and 19. Page 19 was
ads, page 2 seemed to be the human interest page:
a family's problems subsequent to a fire; the re-
union of an aged sister and brother; and the opening of a gay podiatry center. If there was anything
at all pertinent to Frank in this paper, I couldn't
find it.

Glancing quickly through the third plastic bag, I
noted Frank's copies of order forms and corre-
spondence. He had bought liquor weekly, and
other supplies sporadically. There were a few no-
tices from the suppliers acknowledging changes of
amounts, one reminding Frank he had not ordered
at all one week in December, and two more, vir-
tual duplicates of that, dated February 24 and
March 3.

What had I discovered, if anything? There was
no evidence of marijuana. But Frank had to have
been involved in something, if not illegal, at least
clandestine. He didn't buy a bar that had a secret
room just so he would have a spot to store his
heaters and dehumidifier. It was possible that he
had needed the trap door and the access to the
river. But the existence of the trap door was common knowledge in town. So far as I knew, no one
had discovered the secret room.

Still, an empty secret room didn't explain much.
And none of the items I'd found in it were illumi-
nating either. I considered each again: the dish, the
paper, the knob, Frank's financial records; but the
only thing I discovered was that I was too exhausted to think. I stuck the knob and the papers
in a drawer and went to bed.

—I lay on my stomach. The ceiling and the walls of Frank's secret room grew thicker, pushed toward me. The synthetic varnish oozed down the wood, pulling even the air in the secret room into it. I had to strain to breathe. Bells rang. The door shut. All the air was gone. I gasped. The walls were crushing me. The bells rang louder—

I opened my eyes. I was in my own room. It was morning. The pressure I felt came from my own quilt; I was gasping because my head was underneath it. But still I heard the bell. The doorbell.

"Okay," I called as I clambered into my bathrobe and ran my fingers through my hair. It was light out, the muted light of a rainy day. I looked at my watch as I hurried down the stairs to the door. It was nine o'clock, a decent time for anyone who hadn't gone to bed at four-thirty. I felt like I hadn't slept at all.

Let this, I thought as I reached for the door, be someone I can handle quickly—a boy wanting to deliver papers, a civic matron circulating a petition, even a Jehovah's Witness. Two minutes and back to bed. I pulled the door open.

"Good morning, Vejay." Sheriff Wescott stood on the landing, water dripping from his hat.

"Good morning."

"I'd like to talk to you."

"Uh-huh."

"Can I come in?" The rain was soaking his jacket.

"What? Oh, yes, of course. Why don't you go on upstairs to the living room. Give me a couple minutes to wash my face and comb my hair."

"Did I get you up?"

"Yes," I said, hoping he would offer to come

back later. When he didn't, I said, "Sleeping late is one of the few benefits of being suspended from work."

He didn't reply to that either.

As he went upstairs, I stepped into the bathroom, splashed cold water on my face, combed my hair, splashed on more water, dried off, and put on some make-up in a vain attempt to look less pallid and tired. I was barely coherent enough to carry on a normal conversation, much less be interrogated by the sheriff on the morning after I'd broken into Frank's Place. I dabbed witch hazel around my face and headed upstairs.

Wescott was kneeling in front of the fireplace, holding match to newspapers. "I assumed you'd want a fire," he said, turning toward me. "I couldn't find enough newspaper, so I used a couple of your catalogs, too. They were Fall issues."

"That's what they're there for."

"Good."

"How about making some coffee?" he asked. "I've had a long morning while you've been in bed."

"Okay." I could imagine where that long morning had been spent. I didn't want to think why he'd come to discuss it with me. Instead I put the water on and went into the bedroom for a pair of jeans and a sweater. If I was going to be interrogated, at least I should be dressed.

I considered the propriety of making some toast, hesitated, then finally went ahead with it.

Wescott settled against the doorway, watching as I pulled the bread from the toaster. "I've been at Frank's Place this morning, since daybreak."

"Butter?"

"Yes."

"I have peanut butter and jam."

"Butter's fine," he said.

I put two more slices in the toaster.

"Frank's Place was broken into last night," he said.

"Burglarized?"

"It's hard to say if the intruder took anything. I don't know what he, or she, was looking for. I thought maybe you could help me."

"Me? How?"

"You knew Frank well. What might he have had that someone else needed or didn't want anyone else to find?"

I spread butter on the toast. "I have no idea."

"Perhaps something they specifically did not want the sheriff to discover."

The second batch of toast popped up. I jostled the pieces to the plate and spread a pat of butter onto each one. "I would assume if Frank had anything that valuable he would have kept it at his house rather than a spot as public as the Place."

"His house wasn't touched."

I handed Wescott the plate, picked up the mugs of coffee, and walked into the living room by the fire. "What do *you* think it was, Sheriff Wescott?" I sat down.

He leaned an elbow on the mantel, taking his coffee mug in the other hand. "Goulet had a hidden room behind the bar."

"I thought he had a trap door."

"Both."

"What was in this room?" I asked, hoping I was showing the right amount of surprise and natural curiosity.

"Two heaters and a dehumidifier."

"That doesn't sound very secret." Was I being too flip? I wanted to watch his face, but I couldn't because he was keeping an eye on mine.

"Did Frank ever tell you about anything he had that was valuable or incriminating?"

I took a moment to think. It would have been nice to come up with something real. "No."

"Did he ever suggest he was involved in something less than legal, like the drugs you've been talking about?"

"He was no fool. He would hardly have advertised. And no one I've talked to has heard anything about it."

"But he might have told *you*."

"Why me?"

He just stared.

I finished my coffee. "I don't know why I'm bothering to repeat this since it doesn't seem to be getting through to you, but there was nothing between Frank Goulet and me. Zero."

"Where were you last night?"

I covered my gulp by lifting the empty cup to my mouth, then forced a smile. "I was out to dinner, Sheriff, in Jenner, with Ned Jacobs. Ask him, if you like, how much he thinks there was between Frank and me."

It was a definite victory, but temporary. And less likely to throw the sheriff off my track than to move him to consider me in a different light.

He picked up a piece of toast and took a small, thoughtful bite. The toast was cold by now, the butter congealed. A yellow glob stuck between two mustache hairs. "First Goulet's murder," he said almost to himself, "then your truck, and now this. Normally it's only flood waters and burglaries this time of year. We wait in the office till the calls come, then we go to the empty houses—they're almost always empty, either summer places or houses waiting to be sold—we go out and catalog the televisions, stereos, electric typewriters, and now home computers, that are missing. Usually a few radios, maybe some jewelry, but not often when the people aren't living there. Sometimes some valuable decorations, but mostly just the standard electrical equipment."

"Why— Do you want more coffee?"

"Sure."

Picking up his cup, I headed into the kitchen, hopeful that this time he wouldn't follow me. I reheated the water. I had almost asked if Wescott thought Frank were a burglar. Then I remembered the plastic knob. A television knob. Hidden in the secret room. Suddenly it hit me. Frank *was* the burglar, or at least one of the burglars. He wasn't dealing drugs, he was burglarizing.

"Can I help?" Wescott asked as he walked into the kitchen.

"It's only coffee."

"Umm." He made no move to leave. He wasn't going to give me the opportunity to do anything, or even think anything, without his watching.

I turned my back to him, taking my time as I folded the filter paper and wet it before setting it in the holder and adding the ground coffee. Had Frank bought the Place with the idea of moving the burglarized goods along the river and in through the trap door? Televisions, stereos? In canoes, at night? Hardly. The trap door was inessential. Frank had bought the Place for the secret room then, and probably for the location. Closed-up buildings on either side would be a big advantage when moving contraband in and out.

The water boiled. I poured enough to wet the grounds and put the pot back on the stove.

How much could household burglaries bring in in Henderson? It was not something a man who lived in San Francisco, like Frank once did, would think of. Not something that would lure him to drop everything and move to Henderson. Not potentially profitable enough to encourage him to buy the Place.

Trying to sound as if I were making polite conversation while waiting for the water to boil, I said, "I would think there'd be more burglaries now."

"Why?"

"Well, all the new people, all the empty houses."

Wescott laughed. "Maybe a slight rise in the last year or two. But there's only so much work our local burglars want to do. They're just getting better pickings now."

Two years, I thought, the amount of time Frank had been here. I poured enough water nearly to fill the filter paper. There was so much to consider.

Wescott walked back into the living room. The second cup filled up in a minute and, carrying both, I followed him.

He was standing, as before, with one arm leaning on the mantel.

Behind his elbow was the metal dish I took from Frank's.

I lurched forward with the coffee.

"Here." Wescott grabbed for the cups.

"Sorry."

"Did it spill?"

"I don't think so." I took my cup from him. The metal dish! Not just an ashtray. A dish hidden in a secret room. One Frank had stolen. Could it be one of the Chinese bronze plates that had been taken from a summer house here two months ago? What had Madge said about bronze finishes being ruined?

I didn't have time to think about that now. What I needed to do now was to get Wescott out of here before he spotted the dish and made the same connection I had.

But Wescott, leaning on the mantel, waiting for his coffee to cool, looked at home.

"How did you hear that Frank's Place had been broken into?" I asked.

"One of the men discovered it on his rounds."

"What about the old people across the street?"

"They wouldn't have noticed the break-in. That must have been in the middle of the night."

"Haven't you asked them about it?" I demanded.

"We have our procedures."

"The old people across from Frank's seem to escape your procedures with some regularity."

He scowled over his coffee. "Is there something you want to tell me about them?"

"Nothing more than I already have."

He started to put the cup down—on the mantel —but stopped halfway. I could almost see him wonder what had gotten into me.

"Look," I said, "I'm sorry if I'm being inhospitable, but you did wake me up. There are other people you could have seen at nine in the morning,

people who are at work and awake anyway or
retired people who can sleep late every morning.
You may forget that it was your comments that
led to my being suspended. The least you can do is
let me reap the benefits."

"This is a murder investigation."

"Indeed."

"You were friendly with Goulet."

"We've been through all that. I know you don't
believe Frank and I were just friends. There's
nothing more I can tell you to convince you of
that. Repeating your suspicion isn't going to
change it." I walked toward the stairs as I spoke,
drawing his gaze so that his back was to the mantel. I expected him to follow, but he didn't.

I waited.

He made no move.

"Is there another question you intend to ask me,
Sheriff?"

Still he waited, letting his silence take tangible
form. "There's something that you are not telling
me, Vejay, and that is what I want to know."

"And what is that?"

"You tell me."

"I don't know. You're the one who thought this
up."

He waited, then suddenly put the cup down and
walked over to the staircase. "I know you are
withholding information. I . . ." He shrugged
and walked out.

CHAPTER
15

As soon as the door shut behind the sheriff, I raced back upstairs and grabbed the metal dish. Holding it near the lamp, I could make out the hint of curved lines in the center, but the coating of green was so thick it obscured any pattern. The dish had oxidized evenly. It was impossible to tell if the design was Chinese, if the dish was Chinese, or even if it was antique.

Madge Oombs would know. I recalled her telling me about the Japanese bronze buddha. It hadn't taken it long to oxidize. The buddha had been exposed first to humidity and heat, and then to cold. Wrappings had held in the condensation that had formed and the finish was ruined. Similarly, if this dish were one of the Chinese bronze plates, then it had been in the dry warmth of Frank's secret room where the heaters and dehumidifier were on. When the room was opened and the other plates removed, the cold, moisture-laden, outside air had flowed in and remained there to eat away at the plate when the room was resealed.

Madge had told Frank about the Japanese buddha. So Frank would have realized the need to protect the finish on the plates with the heaters and the dehumidifier.

Madge would require only one look to decide if

this were one of the Chinese set, but she was hardly someone I could ask. What could I say, Madge, can you tell me about this dish I stole from Frank's Place last night? Would you mind not mentioning it to the sheriff?

I picked up the sheet of newspaper again, checking every article, then reading each one, all the while knowing that my first conclusion would be borne out: nothing printed here related to the burglaries or the bronze plate. Still, I didn't toss the paper in the fire. I folded it and put it under the plate.

The knob took less time. Now that I suspected it was from a television, I wondered why I hadn't realized that sooner. It was a standard plastic television knob, the type used to adjust the color. As such, it was not an item that would be missed immediately, like an on-off knob or a channel selector. Had the owner of the bronze dishes also lost a television? Or was this from a different haul?

I took out the papers I'd found in Frank's cabinet and arranged them chronologically, noting Frank's weekly orders for liquor and mixers, his monthly bills for laundry and paper products. I put the letters that reminded him he had not submitted orders in their proper places by date. Frank had been relatively organized, which didn't surprise me. He had bought approximately the same quantity of goods each week. He had forgotten to order once before Christmas, a time when many things are overlooked, and twice more recently, within the last two months. After stealing a valuable set of Chinese plates, forgetting to order beer, wine, and mixers was understandable.

I was definitely going to have to find out about

the plate. The library in Guerneville would have the old newspaper clippings, perhaps with photos clear enough to link this plate to the set.

I took one last long look at the plate, grabbed my slicker, and headed for the door.

A sheriff's car was parked across the street.

It could have been a coincidence, but I'd never seen a sheriff's car there before.

Leaving the door open, I went back inside, gathered two library books, and headed back out.

The rain had stopped, but the sky was still gunmetal gray. It seemed to hang like a wet canvas from invisible hooks just above the treetops, ready to fall on the earth whenever one of those hooks would no longer hold.

I made my way down the fifty-two steps, relieved that they were all still there, all still steady. My pickup truck was in the service station in Guerneville, repaired (I hoped) and waiting.

As I came abreast of the sheriff's car, I tapped on the window. The young deputy at the wheel jerked his attention from the rear-view mirror and rolled down the window.

"I'm going to the library in Guerneville," I said. "I wondered if you could take me."

He was blond with pinkish skin. He looked decidedly uncomfortable. "What? The taxi service—"

"My truck is in the shop. It's a long walk."

"I see. But I don't—"

"My name is Vejay Haskell. Sheriff Wescott had my truck towed there. I'm sure he would want to help me get it back. You can call and ask him."

He stared, then nodded, and rolled up the window. The call took little more than a minute, after which he motioned me in the back, behind the wire mesh.

"I'm going to the library," I repeated, "but you might as well drop me at the service station for my truck."

He said nothing as he started the car, and nothing on the drive into Guerneville, and nothing as I thanked him and got out.

The truck, of course, wasn't quite ready. Another half hour, the manager said. They could do the billing now, though.

Normally, I wouldn't have put pen to check before seeing my truck, but today I went ahead, took possession of the numerous forms, and waited to have my check okayed. When the procedures were completed, the truck still needed another half an hour.

The sheriff's car was outside. I waved and mouthed "not ready" as I passed. I walked down the main street, stopping at the bakery for a donut. The rain-free day had brought out everyone in town. The sidewalks were crowded and people pushed their way in and out of every shop.

The library was behind the main part of town, away from the river. The book-drop was full; there was no one at the check-out counter.

The librarian had copies of the *San Francisco Chronicle* for the last three months and issues of the local papers dating back one year. Earlier than that, I would have to do my research on microfilm.

I started with the local paper on the premise that the coverage of the theft would be big news here, be an item of interest in Santa Rosa, and barely merit mention in the San Francisco paper.

An hour later I realized that my assessment had been only partly right. The local paper was indeed thorough—to the point of repetitiveness—so that it took me nearly an entire hour to read its coverage, only to discover that after the first week no new facts were reported. But I dared not skip over it. The *Chronicle,* however, had given this out-of-town theft greater space than I had foreseen because the owner of the Chinese plates was a Martin Walucyk, an art collector and part-time professor who lived mainly in San Francisco. Together the papers explained that Walucyk had purchased a house in Henderson three years ago as a summer and weekend retreat. As a collector he sometimes brought valuable items there, and therefore had a temperature/humidity-controlled case in the house, where he kept the Chinese plates. Along with the plates, the usual range of electrical equipment had been taken in the burglary. The sheriff had no clues as to the identity of the culprits, but said that burglaries of empty dwellings had been a problem throughout the Russian River area. What neither paper contained was a distinguishable picture of the plates to tell me whether mine had been one of them.

To discover that, I would need to see Walucyk.

And he, of course, would be in San Francisco. I was here at the library; my truck was four blocks away; and the sheriff's deputy sat outside. I could hardly have a deputy tail me to Walucyk's house.

I couldn't creep through Guerneville with the ease which I'd covered Henderson last night. Certainly not at midday.

I glanced out the window. The sheriff's car was across the street.

The library did have a back door behind the check-out counter, a private door for the staff. I walked over to the counter and looked in its direction.

"Can I help you?" the librarian asked. She was about my age. She looked familiar, as most people in this area did. I'd taken a class with one, chatted with another in the market, or failing that, read their meter.

The library was empty now but for the second librarian in the back room. I said to the woman at the desk. "I need to ask you a big favor. Not money," I added quickly.

She smiled warily.

"My truck's at the garage. I feel truly lousy. I just can't face the walk across town. I know it's asking a lot, I mean we hardly know each other— weren't you in the film class at the college last year?"

"Right. I thought I knew you."

"Anyway, I wondered if you could drive me to my truck. I'd really appreciate it."

She hesitated, looking around at the empty room. "I guess so. We're not exactly crowded today. Georgia can handle any rush in the next five minutes. Come on, my car's out back."

I followed her through the office, out the rear door, and into an ancient blue Pontiac. From there it was easy to direct her out the right-hand exit, the one farthest from the deputy. I thought he glanced at the car, but if so she was between him and me. And in any case he didn't move. At the garage, I thanked her, hopped out, collected the keys for my truck, and drove off.

When I was buying the truck, my personal statement of country life, I had eyed a bright red model. The friend I took with me laughed. "A little red wagon?" he asked. Reluctantly, I agreed that it was a bit much, and in reaction bought the plainest one in the lot, the brown. But now as I drove through town, garnering no notice at all, I silently thanked him. Maybe when this was all over I'd have him over to dinner. And the woman from the library. And all the people in Henderson I'd offended. I'd have to rent a hall.

I made it to Route 101 in reasonable time. North Bank Road was crowded. I didn't want to speed, but on 101 I felt safe. Here I was no longer Vejay Haskell of Henderson, but an anonymous Californian driving along one of the main north-south freeways.

I stopped looking in the rear-view mirror and considered how I would approach Walucyk.

The *Chronicle* referred to his address only as "in Pacific Heights," an old moneyed section of San Francisco. But our local paper, less sophisticated, or less concerned about the privacy of city folk, had given it out, street and number. Both papers carried a description of the plates, a set of ten antique bronze religious plates, decreasing in size from forty inches in diameter to five (mine, presumably). Etched into each one was an ancient religious symbol. They were valued at three hundred thousand dollars. A very lucky find for Frank.

Or as it turned out, very unlucky.

A four-color article in the *Chronicle*, which originally ran during the time Walucyk bought the plates (and was reprinted after the burglary news thinned), reviewed Walucyk's history as a collector, listing several coups which had astounded fellow art lovers. In fact, his discovery and purchase of the Chinese bronze plates aroused jealousy as far away as England. The report quoted a Professor Everson of Leeds University in England as saying his school had eyed the plates soon after China had been reopened to the West, but Walucyk had beaten them to it. Everson had made Walucyk an offer for the plates (amount unspecified in the article) and was rejected.

As I headed across the Golden Gate Bridge, I wondered if Frank could have been on the payroll of this Professor Everson. It was farfetched. But then Frank's death still seemed unreal.

I stopped at the toll gate. The sky was overcast, but compared to the Russian River area, it was almost bright. I drove past the sailboats in the marina and turned right, up into Pacific Heights, hoping Walucyk would be home.

When I found his house, a beautiful plum-accented blue and beige Victorian, a Mercedes was pulling out of the driveway.

CHAPTER
16

On the drive over to the city I had considered how to approach Walucyk. A man who had recently lost his prized Chinese plates might not be anxious to invite a strange woman into his house to view his remaining collection. What would reassure him? Getting inside someone's house had never been a problem for me. When I worked in the city my clients were always anxious for my help. In Henderson I simply showed my PG&E identification.

After rejecting several possibilities, I recalled a friend, a freelance writer who did articles "on spec." She'd phone and say "I'm writing an article on spec for *West Coast* magazine . . ." "On spec," she explained, meant not requested by the magazine. But the prospective interviewee never noted the "on spec," only the *West Coast* magazine. Secondly, she added, interviews were much easier to get than one might think. People liked to talk about their work; they loved to talk about themselves; and they adored the idea that others were waiting to read about their favorite subject.

I'd see.

I jumped out of the truck and ran to the Mercedes. Tapping on the driver's window, I said, "Mr. Walucyk?"

The man, middle-aged, small, and almost completely bald, rolled the window down half an inch. "Yes?"

"Are you Martin Walucyk?"

"Yes."

"I'm Merle Dubrow. I tried to call you. I'm writing an article on spec for *West Coast* magazine about Asian art collections and art collectors. I'll only be in San Francisco today. I would really like to talk to you."

He hesitated, then nodded, closed the window, and pulled the Mercedes back up the driveway.

The house was square, large, three stories. The doorway faced the drive. Approaching the hulking dwelling, Walucyk looked even smaller. He was perhaps five feet four. As with many bald men he looked as if his head had been spun violently and all his features resettled together by centrifugal force, leaving large areas of untenanted skin. His pate had a muted shine. His suit was brown, the turtleneck under it camel. It looked expensive, befitting the owner of the house and the Mercedes.

Using two keys Walucyk opened the door, then, motioning for me to wait, he adjusted several switches on the wall.

It seemed ridiculous to invest in such security if he had the habit of inviting people in off the street.

I followed him into the living room, a large room created by merging the front and rear parlors. It was darkly panelled, a room that no amount of sunshine could brighten. The floors were covered with oriental carpets; the sofas, loveseats, and chairs reminded me of the furnishings of minor European palaces open to the public. These were not pieces that invited one to sit down.

Against each of the walls were lighted cases, each holding display collections. For a moment I forgot my purpose as I stared at the elaborate and delicate ivory carving of a small hillside village. The whole work was no more than a foot high. "Amazing," I said.

"It's thirteenth-century Japanese. From Hokkaido. It does look amazing even to those who know nothing of Asian carvings. But experts have seen and agreed that the craftsmanship was exceptionally subtle for so early a period."

I nodded, not knowing what to say.

But there was no need for response. Walucyk motioned me to another display case. In it were six rice paper fans edged with gold. "These, you may not realize, are from the Tang Dynasty in China. From the court, of course. No one has seen anything like it here since the Boxer Rebellion. A few amateurs tried to get Chinese artifacts when the country reopened, but all they got was junk. One of those men, a dealer,"—he emitted the word rather like a noxious gas—"even saw these and passed them by. Looking for something flashier, no doubt. I spotted them instantly, and if I do say so, got an exceptional deal."

I nodded again.

"Over here are my smallest carvings. Even the museums have some of these netsukes. Japanese work has been easier to come by. Of course, the museums are inclined to the less subtle. But their budgets are limited."

And their visitors peasants, I was tempted to say. For such a little man, Walucyk was certainly one big pain in the ass.

In the corner was an empty display case. I

walked toward it. "Was this where you kept the Chinese dishes?" That would be a reasonable question from a writer.

"Devotional plates," he corrected.

"Devotional plates."

"But that is what you've come to discuss, isn't it? Do you realize that that particular set is nearly five hundred years old. Before the present revolution those plates were kept in places of honor in the temple and used as vessels during sacred ceremonies to contact ancestors."

"They were used outside, exposed to the atmosphere?" I said, amazed.

Had Walucyk been taller he would have looked down his nose at me. "The city was in the mountains. The air was dry, the area arid. Perfect conditions for preservation. Many people don't realize that much of China is mountainous and dry. Even in our own country many people fail to understand why parchments are preserved better in Arizona than New Hampshire."

"Could you describe the plates?" I said, anxious to get on with it.

He looked surprised. "Yes, I suppose so. They are a set of ten, which in itself is extraordinary. The normal religious set would be nine. With these, the tenth was made for good luck."

"Sort of 'one to grow on'?" I was sorry as soon as I said it.

Walucyk ignored my comment. "Each plate has the temple insignia in the center. The set, as you know, is bronze, and also," he said, gazing at me almost in supplication, "as you know, oxidizes rapidly without proper care."

"Do you have a picture of them?"

"A picture? Why do you want to see that?"

"I may want to illustrate my article," I said.

Walucyk tensed. "Very well. The photographic work is over here." He removed a portfolio of twelve-by-fourteen photographs from a cabinet and laid it on a table, turning plastic-enclosed pages of photos until he came to one showing the ten plates. The photo was in color. The plates glistened green-gold in the light. The design so muted on my own little dish showed up strong and clear here. And it looked the same. I was struck by the beauty of the plates in their original condition. I hoped the other nine had fared better than mine.

"Is the design unusual?"

He looked surprised and annoyed.

"I mean, would this be the only set of plates with this design?"

"Of course. It is the temple insignia."

"And you bought them right after China was reopened?"

"As I said, I knew what I was doing. Many men pay too much or sell too cheaply, and then they are put out. That is their own fault. I know my field."

"I understand a Professor Everson wanted to buy them from you."

He closed the portfolio. "Could we get on with this, Miss, er, Dubrow?"

He seemed so annoyed now that I wondered if he was beginning to doubt that I was really a writer. "Certainly," I said. "I will remember what you've told me so far. It all seems very clear, but perhaps it would be best if I did take some notes now." I took a pad from my purse. "What are the joys and the sorrows of being a collector?"

"You mean, how did I feel when these plates were stolen?"

I nodded, delighted with his choice of response.

"As even you might expect, I was worried for their safety and enraged over the theft."

"You didn't feel any danger in taking them to your Russian River home?"

"Surely . . ." He shrugged. "As I told the sheriff and the state police, a colleague of Professor Everson's called, a man named Smithson. Or so he said. He said he worked for a collector in London and would be interested in seeing the plates. He mentioned that as a Londoner he was always delighted to get out of the city. So I suggested he come to my weekend house. It had a display case. That was one of the reasons I bought that particular house: there was a display case already installed. I bought the house from a friend who kept Egyptian work."

"And this Smithson?"

"I was to meet him at the Santa Rosa Airport Saturday morning, at seven. He said he was flying in from Portland." He paused. "Surely we can skip this."

I hesitated to push him. Still I said, "I do need to know."

Again he shrugged. "As you say. I guess I have no choice. I drove to Henderson Friday night and brought the devotional plates into the house. When I went to the airport Saturday morning, I left the crates stacked right beside the devotional plates," he said in disgust. "Of course, there was no Smithson on the flight. By the time I checked with the airline and found that Smithson had not merely missed the flight, but had never had a seat on it, over an hour had elapsed. I called the number Smithson had given me. There was no Smithson there. Everson never heard of him. And when I got back to the house the plates were gone. Is that sufficient?"

"Originally, had Smithson written you or called?"

"He called. Do we really need—"

"Did he have an English accent?"

"No. He said he was raised in Canada."

"So, you assume Smithson was connected with the theft," I said.

Walucyk nodded in disgust.

"What about local connections in the Russian River area. Who are you familiar with there?"

Walucyk seemed about to retort, but instead swallowed, and with enforced calm, said, "I have neither the time nor the inclination to consort with the locals."

"You don't go to restaurants or bars there?"

"Restaurants, yes. I must eat. But only the Johnson House. Bars hardly."

The Johnson House was far beyond my means. It was located east of Guerneville. "Are you saying you've never been to a bar or restaurant other than the Johnson House?"

"That," he sighed, "is what I am saying."

"What about repair work on your home, or plumbing, or carpentry? You must have had some work done."

"If you're trying to figure out what I told the sheriff, I'll tell you. I don't know anything more than the obvious. I told the sheriff what I knew. The sheriff did nothing for me. My main concern is my devotional plates."

"So you didn't have work done on the house?"

"No. Nothing. It was in good shape when I bought it. That was only three years ago. I spend enough money keeping *this* place in repair."

I made a show of jotting down his comment. "One last thing: have you been contacted by the thieves?"

Walucyk stared at me. "Of course. Twice."

"And those times were . . . ?"

He gave me the same annoyed and confused look. "I don't know why . . . but whatever you say. The first time was a week after the theft."

"A man called you?"

"Yes," he said, still looking at me with disgust. "A man."

"What did he say?"

"Three hundred thousand dollars. He told me to pay it if I planned on seeing the plates again."

"Did he say what he would do if you didn't pay?"

"I didn't ask."

"And did you agree?"

"As you know," he said slowly, apparently using considerable control, "I said I'd have to see if I could raise it."

Involuntarily, I glanced around the room.

"Possessions are not cash," he snapped. "Raising three hundred thousand dollars takes time."

"Did you get the money?"

"For all the good . . ." He compressed his hands into fists.

I waited.

He did likewise.

Finally, I said, "What do you mean 'For all the good . . .'? Hasn't the thief called back?"

"Oh yes. He called."

"When?"

"He called this week."

"This week! When?"

"Monday. At two-seventeen in the afternoon."

The afternoon Frank was murdered. "What did he say?" The excitement rang clear in my voice.

"Four hundred thousand dollars."

"What? You mean he raised the price?"

"That's what I said."

"That doesn't make sense."

His hands squeezed tighter.

"Did he say why?"

"He said, Miss, er, Dubrow, that he had changed his mind. I could take it or leave it. I told him he'd never fence the plates. He laughed. He said that wasn't my affair. I need only concern myself with whether I wanted to see them again or not. But you know all that."

"No."

"Let's not play games."

I decided to let that one pass. "You talked to the same man both times. Just one man?"

Walucyk hesitated.

"There was more than one man?" I prompted.

"Yes and no. There was a voice in the background the second time."

"A man?"

"I don't know. Oh God, I shouldn't have said anything. It was just a voice. Believe me, I couldn't identify it. Just sounds." He looked terrified. "Look, I just want my collection back."

"But what did the thief say? Was he going to contact you again?"

"By this weekend. He said he'd be in touch."

For the first time he looked directly at me. "I have the money. I told him I didn't have it. But I do now. All the money. I'll pay the four hundred thousand. But I can't get more. I've borrowed all I can. This is it." All Walucyk's condescension had vanished. He looked like all the ransom victims I'd ever seen on the news. I was glad I wasn't going to be here when the week ended and Frank didn't call back.

There was nothing more to say. I closed my pad. "Well, thank you for your time, Mr. Walucyk. You've been a great help to me in writing my article. And I hope your plates will be returned to you very soon."

"Is that all?" He sounded amazed.

"Yes, but thanks again."

"I will be called . . ."

"I'm sure—"

"I want the devotional plates. I've done what you said."

Suddenly I realized Walucyk thought I was one of the thieves. He assumed I was the contact he was expecting. No wonder he had been so cooperative, and so bewildered. I opened my mouth to tell him I was innocent, then shut it. Walucyk wouldn't believe me. Nothing I could say would convince him now.

"Be patient," I said, and headed for the door. Walucyk followed me. Stopping at the doorway, I said, "Go into the dining room and wait there for five minutes. You understand?"

He nodded.

He opened the front door. I passed through, careful not to touch the brass knob, and ran down the driveway.

I couldn't spot a head in the living room window as I started the truck. If Walucyk had obeyed me, my truck and my licence plates would be out of his line of sight. If not, I was in a lot of trouble.

CHAPTER

17

I had a lot of time to think on the way home. By Route 101 the drive to Henderson takes a little more than two hours. But not knowing whether Walucyk had seen my truck and then notified the highway patrol, I was afraid to cross the Golden Gate Bridge. It would be easy to spot a vehicle here.

I rather doubted if Walucyk had called anyone. He seemed more concerned about recovering his plates than in promoting justice. My guess was that he would spend a few days, a week, maybe even two, hoping to hear from the thieves again.

Of course, Walucyk didn't know that the main thief was dead. He didn't know Frank was the thief, so even if he had seen the news coverage of Frank's murder it would mean nothing to him. Unless he killed Frank.

Suddenly that seemed to be a surprising and rather appealing thought. In the back of my mind, carefully unacknowledged, was the fear that Frank's killer was one of my friends. I didn't deal with it because there seemed to be no other alternatives. But Walucyk, that smug little snob who condescended to dine at a restaurant I couldn't even afford, would be a great find as Frank's killer. I certainly wouldn't miss him. It was surprising how much he had irritated me in so short a time.

I laughed out loud. I had thought I was deceiving Walucyk. I had congratulated myself for gaining access to his house and his collections, for saying just the right thing—Miss "On-Spec" Writer. I could have given him any story. He thought I was one of the thieves. It didn't matter what I'd said.

Deciding against the safest and the longest route home (south to San Jose and looping back on the far side of the bay), I made a compromise and headed east across the Bay Bridge to Oakland, then drove north from there.

Once on the bridge, I went over what exactly I had learned from Walucyk. He was certainly an obnoxious little man. But could he be a killer? I wasn't sure. He didn't strike me as one who would have second thoughts over employing an assassin once he was assured of his own safety. But hiring a third party is always dangerous. Walucyk did not seem like a man who would readily accept danger, certainly not one who would creep unseen into the Place and shoot Frank with his own gun. His Mercedes parked outside Frank's would have been noticed by more than the old people across the street, and the alternative—Walucyk canoeing to Frank's trap door—was too ridiculous to consider.

So, onward to the motive.

Suppose Walucyk and Frank were partners.

To steal Walucyk's own property?

Well, no. But perhaps to simulate a theft and defraud Walucyk's insurance company. A set of three hundred thousand dollar plates had to be insured. So suppose Walucyk had met Frank in San Francisco and set him up in Henderson with

he secret room, and then had Frank steal the
plates and hide them there. Then Frank wouldn't
give them back for the price they had agreed
upon?

I sighed. There were plenty of holes in that theory. First, there was no reason to think Frank and
Walucyk knew each other. San Francisco is a big
place. Even an interest in Asian art does not imply
knowing every other aficionado in the business.
And Frank wasn't in Walucyk's league. The set of
Chinese plates was merely one of Walucyk's collections. He probably had over half a million dollars' worth of art in his living room alone. When
Frank lived in the city, he had to sell his ivory just
to meet the rent.

Secondly, even if Walucyk had met Frank and
planned an insurance fraud, he would have had no
way of knowing if there was a bar with a secret
room for sale in Henderson.

Lastly, if Walucyk had picked someone to steal
his collection, he wouldn't have chosen a man
whose sole vehicle was a red sports car with so
little room to carry anything that it would have
required two trips to do the job.

No, it was much more reasonable to accept
Walucyk for what he was: a rich, obnoxious collector whose Chinese plates had been stolen.
Therefore, what he told me was also likely to be
true.

Monday afternoon at two-seventeen, two hours
after I had stalked out of the place, Frank called
Walucyk to raise the ransom price. Someone was
with him. Frank would hardly have anyone other
than his partner there at that time. And the part-

ner would have had the vehicle to transport th
plates.

I drove north now, through Hercules, and
Crockett, and across the Carquinez Bridge. A
soon as I left the city the San Francisco mist turned
to rain and was coming down heavily. I switched
the wipers to high.

So in the process of one of their housebreaking
Frank and his partner stumbled upon the Chinese
plates. Perhaps Frank, familiar with oriental art
recognized the plates. What was it Chris said
about Frank? Frank hated to be taken, and once
he became interested in something he researched i
thoroughly. But that was only after the item
caught his attention. So he probably didn't know
anything about the plates before he stole them.

Maybe his partner was the knowledgeable one
Madge, as I thought earlier this morning, migh
well have studied about Chinese bronze. Skip.
Maybe, though he never said anything to sugges
it. Paul and Patsy? Rosa, Carlo, Chris? Ned? I
couldn't imagine any of them knowing a Chinese
devotional plate from a brass candy dish.

I veered left and headed northwest, back toward
the ocean. I was still well east of Henderson, still
thirty miles southeast of Santa Rosa.

There was one other possibility, an accomplice
who would be familiar with a Chinese ceremonia
plate, one who had access to a truck, and whose
truck could be seen around town without raising
suspicion: the Chinese Laundry.

The Chinese Laundry truck came to Frank'
Place daily. The driver could have carted contra
band in or out. He could have stopped anywhere
on his route. If the truck had been parked outside

Walucyk's Russian River house, it might not have been noticed. It certainly wasn't spotted outside Frank's Place the day he was killed, at least not by the old people across the street.

The Chinese Laundry building was in Santa Rosa. It was four-thirty now, but I didn't picture the owners of a Chinese laundry knocking off early. I envisioned them standing over their machines, thinking, in Chinese, about the ceremonial plates.

Even if they did not recognize the plates themselves, a Chinese person might be alerted by the insignia. Through benevolent associations or family ties, they would probably be able to discover the origin of the plates and their worth.

Perhaps Frank's partner objected to ransoming the plates. Perhaps the plates were of such religious significance that he did not want them out of Chinese hands once they had come into his possession. Was that the reason Frank was killed?

Or perhaps the partner was willing to surrender the plates to occidental hands only for a higher ransom price—four hundred thousand dollars instead of three. Then, when Walucyk balked, Frank might well have suspected the whole deal would fall through. He might have realized that Walucyk would contact the sheriff and the state police, and not only would he get nothing for the plates, but even his regular housebreaking would become much more difficult and dangerous. Certainly an argument over that could have led to Frank's death.

And, the fact was that the Chinese Laundry truck was at Frank's Place after I left there Monday. The driver of the laundry truck didn't have to

slink along South Bank Road or battle the river
currents in a canoe. He only had to walk into the
Place, as he did daily, and shoot Frank.

I turned onto the Santa Rosa business loop. I'd
seen the laundry building when I substituted for a
Santa Rosa meter reader months ago. It was only
two blocks off the freeway.

As I pulled into the driveway, I noted six trucks
parked alongside the building. I pulled in, jumped
down from the cab, and headed for the office.

On the door, under the name CHINESE LAUNDRY
was a drawing of a hand with the tips of the
thumb and first finger meeting. Inside the circle
formed was a Chinese pictogram, similar to ones
used in pendants, which stands for good luck,
long life, or wealth. Taking this as a good omen, I
opened the door.

The office was empty except for a woman who
sat behind a desk. The laundry handled commercial accounts only, so there was no need for a
counter; the napkins and tablecloths were brought
in off the trucks.

"Can I help you?" The woman looked up. She
was small, blond, and definitely not Chinese. She
was also in the process of stuffing something into
her purse. I glanced at the clock above her. It was
two minutes to five.

"I'm looking for the owner."

"Is there a problem?"

"I need to speak to him."

"Our customer service representative—"

"I have to speak to the owner."

She hesitated, then said, "I'm sorry, Mr. Fitzgerald is in Reno."

"Fitzgerald!"

"Yes, Mr. James J. Fitzgerald."

"But this is the Chinese Laundry."

She laughed. I could tell my reaction was not unique.

"It is," she said. "Mr. Fitzgerald bought it from the Wu family four years ago. He left the name because"—she eyed me appraisingly—"because how many people are going to send their linens to something called the Irish Laundry? That sounds like something that handles I.R.A. funds."

"What about drivers? Do you have any Chinese drivers?"

"No." She looked pointedly at the clock. It was after five. "The drivers will be around back now. You can see for yourself, if you go quickly."

"Thanks." I hurried out.

The rain was heavy; the parking lot dotted with puddles. Frank's partner didn't have to be the owner of the laundry; he only needed to be the driver on that route. He didn't even have to be Chinese. Walucyk wasn't Chinese and he was an expert on Asian art.

By the time I got out back I could see three pickup trucks pulling out, two men talking, and another climbing into a Honda. None of the three were Chinese.

I approached the two standing together. One pulled open the door of an old Chevy and climbed in. The other leaned over to the window and said something; I was still too far away to hear.

"Excuse me," I said, coming up beside him. "Are any of the drivers here Chinese?"

He turned. "What?"

"Chinese. Are any of the drivers Chinese?"

"Nope. Not a one. Not in the three years I've

worked here. You seen any Chinese here, Sam?"
he asked the man in the Chevy. The man shook his
head.

"Who drives the route in Henderson?" I asked
the man outside.

"Why do you want to know?"

"I need to talk to him."

He was middle-aged, a bit given to paunch, and
a lot given to trailing brown hair. Without moving
his head he looked me up and down. "I guess you
can talk to me."

"You mean you're the Henderson driver?"

"As much as anyone."

"Huh?" The rain was smacking on my face. I
had to shout.

"We rotate. Fitzgerald's Rule. We never know
what route we'll be doing until we get to work,
see? Pain in the ass, but that's what the boss
wants."

"How come?"

"Well, you know."

"No."

He looked me square in the face, then shrugged.
"There was some trouble a couple of years ago.
One of the drivers had his own route, if you know
what I mean—his own deliveries. Sheriff didn't
like that. Boss didn't like it either."

"Gotcha," I said. "And thanks."

"Hey," he called as I started off.

I turned back.

"You want to come for a drink?" he called.

"Another time. Thanks."

By the time I ran to the truck, I was soaked,
tired, hungry, depressed, and angry. I was all those

things the sign on the door of the ersatz-Chinese laundry was not.

When I considered Frank's murder, the Chinese Laundry truck was always an element. It seemed important. How could it be so expendable?

But since there were no Chinese, art experts or not, driving the trucks or in ownership positions, and no drivers on the route long enough or reliably enough to be useful to Frank, then the only reason that the Chinese Laundry truck was at Frank's Place the day Frank was killed was to deliver laundry.

I backed my own pickup out, pulled onto the road, and headed toward Henderson. In the glove compartment were chocolate bars I kept for emergencies. Added to the toast I'd had at breakfast and the donut later, the chocolate bar would complete a diet I was glad my mother wasn't aware of.

I realized as I crossed the freeway that I was depressed not only because a promising lead had evaporated, but that in its loss, I had eliminated another chance for Frank's killer to be a stranger. Like Martin Walucyk, someone at the Chinese Laundry would have made a very acceptable perpetrator. Now I was left with only my friends to suspect.

Not wanting to think about it, I turned on the radio. Waylon Jennings sang a few bars, then faded off.

"The big news here in Russian River country is the river itself. According to unofficial reports the river is expected to crest at Cloverdale late tomorrow morning. As the water rushes downstream the other towns along its banks continue to prepare for the worst." This was a local station. As the flood neared, I'd been told, high water reports were broadcast on the hour, then on the half-hour, then every fifteen minutes, till the flood water washed out the electricity. "Residents of Guerneville," the announcer continued, "should expect the river to flood by tomorrow afternoon."

I turned the report off. At least North Bank Road shouldn't be under water now.

In the silence I ran through the revelations of the day. Frank had a partner. It could be any of those who'd been at Rosa's eating fettucini the night of Frank's death. Every one of us had a suitable vehicle. But one had to be the prime suspect. Who?

Belying the radio report, water covered portions of the road. I slowed, spraying a passing car as I drove by.

Lights were on in the houses on the hillside. Those buildings between the road and the river were dark, deserted. When the river flooded tomorrow the whole Russian River area would be like those houses, except instead of emptiness there would be confusion. There would be enough mud and water and panic to thwart any sleuthing I had in mind, and to cover any moves the killer chose to make. If I were to find Frank's killer before he'd covered his tracks forever, I'd have to do it while the river was still between its banks.

Which of us was closer to Frank? Who knew something? Who acted different around him? Who was especially upset at the time of his murder?

Frank gave the impression of being everyone's friend. But there was only one person he met regularly. There was only one person he saw twice a month, deliberately, out of view from the casual observer. Only one person he met intentionally in the state park.

I crossed the bridge to South Bank Road and headed to the canoe rental.

There had been puddles in the parking lot of Paul and Patsy Fernandez's canoe rental when I'd left there two days ago. I'd had trouble avoiding the potholes. Now heading through it was more like steering a boat than driving a truck. The water splashed at the doors of the pickup. Twice I drove into a pothole and had to gun the engine to keep going. The canoe rental was on low ground, almost in the river at the best of times. It flooded early, dried late. Had it been run by anyone other than Paul and Patsy, I would have been surprised to see a light in the office window. (Of course, if someone else were running it, they would not be living in the office.)

Even in boots and rain gear I wasn't prepared for the wade over to the office door. The water topped my boots and soaked my jeans. I knocked hard on the door.

Paul opened it. "Hi, Vejay, how're things? Sheriff leaving you alone?" he asked before it occurred to him to move aside and let me in. In my haste to confront Patsy I hadn't considered what to do about Paul. Frank's meetings had been with Patsy alone. No one had observed him talking to Paul. It was very possible that Paul was entirely innocent of their arrangement, in which case Patsy was not likely to talk in front of him.

"You're soaking," Paul said.

"No other way to get here."

"Yeah, well," he said, as if those two words were an explanation. "How about some brandy to warm you up? We still have a little."

"Thanks."

Patsy was sitting on the leather sofa, her long black hair falling over the thick cowl of a wool sweater and the collar of a down jacket. She had a blanket pulled around her legs. She merely nodded in my direction.

For the first time I noticed the kerosene lamps, four of them, burning in groups of twos. "How long has your power been off?" I asked her.

"Since noon. It's a bummer."

"Cold," I said.

"Cold and boring. No music. No television. All you can do is think about how cold you are."

Paul handed me a glass and took another to Patsy. The discussion of temperature reminded me that my wet jeans were becoming icy. The heat of the brandy going down my throat felt good. If only it could travel to my feet.

"Why don't you leave?" I asked. "Park your van on high ground, or go to one of the shelters. It's only going to get worse here."

"Can't," Paul said, sitting on the couch next to Patsy and pulling the blanket over his legs.

I waited.

It was Patsy who explained. "We don't dare go because of the canoes. The lock's broken on the main door. Anyone could take them."

"Very few people are thinking of canoeing right now," I said.

"There's always someone looking for the main

chance." Paul swallowed a fair amount of his brandy. I was surprised the bottle had lasted this long.

Brandy glass in hand, Paul did not look uncomfortable under the blanket. I suspected he'd lived in more primitive conditions than this and was resigned to waiting out the worst.

I said, "You know the sheriff's been questioning me."

"Uh-huh." Paul leaned forward. Patsy didn't move.

"He was by today."

"And?"

"Well, he really didn't know anything new, except that Frank's Place had been broken into."

Paul leaned even farther forward. But Patsy showed no sign of interest.

"The sheriff doesn't have any idea why," I said. "Or at least if he does, he wasn't telling me."

"They never tell you anything. They try to catch you, see what you know," Paul said.

"Right," I agreed. "But what he did ask was if I would be seeing you."

Both of them looked surprised and wary.

"I said I might."

Paul nodded, still cautious.

"He needs to talk to you about the canoes."

Their relief was obvious.

"Tonight."

When Paul didn't move, I embellished the lie by adding, "I spoke to him this morning, so he expected you earlier than this. You'd better go now. At least it'll be warm there."

Paul hesitated, but Patsy didn't. She gave him a shove.

"Bring some more brandy on your way back," she said.

"And I'll see what kind of money I can get up front this year." To me, he added, "You know the county didn't pay anything for the canoes last year."

"I know."

Since he was wearing virtually everything he owned, it took Paul no time to get ready to leave. He threw on a slicker, stepped into his boots, and was gone.

I waited till I heard the van drive off before saying to Patsy, "Tell me about the illegal business you and Frank had."

She stared at me, silently.

"You and Frank met, sometimes in town, more frequently in the state park. You were seen."

Still she didn't speak.

"You were very upset when Frank was killed, much more so than the people who had been his friends for years."

She sipped her brandy, looking down into the glass as she drank.

"This boat rental is a marginal business, as Paul has said many times. But across from you is a new television, on that wall"—I gestured at the wall to her left—"is a stereo system that cost plenty. The floor is covered with an oriental carpet. You're sitting on a real leather couch. And your boots alone cost more than you earn in a week."

"So?"

"So, the money came from the illegal venture you and Frank had going. You can tell me about it, or you can tell the sheriff."

I expected the threat of the sheriff to suffice, but

Patsy didn't crumble. She pulled the blanket tighter around her and said, "Possessing material goods isn't a crime. Meeting with friends is legal. What is this scoop you're going to give the sheriff, Vejay?"

"I'll tell him, Patsy, that you came here with nothing. Both you and Frank lived in the city. Frank had a burglary ring going. He worked with a partner, a partner who had a van to cart off the goods. And you are that partner."

"That's supposition."

"Maybe so. Let the sheriff worry about that. He can dig into your life till he finds hard facts."

She shrugged. "Let him." But the words didn't carry much bravado.

I stood up, prepared to play out her bluff.

She sat.

I reached for the door.

Patsy remained motionless, but her face had lost its cool indifference.

Suddenly I realized this silence was her defense. I wouldn't break through that by threatening to leave.

I yanked her up off the sofa and thrust her hard against the wall. She gasped.

"The sheriff is on my tail, and I'm good and sick of it," I said. "Either you tell me exactly, every detail of what you and Frank were up to or . . ."

Her breath came quick; her eyes looked too wide for her face. Still, she didn't speak.

"I'm strong, Patsy, and I'm desperate. You tell me—now."

"Okay." The word was so small and breathless it was barely audible.

I loosened my grip.

Patsy's eyes were wide, her breath still taut. "Okay," she repeated. "But I don't know anything about any burglaries."

I tightened my hands on her jacket.

"That's the truth, Vejay. Frank may have been heisting stuff, but he didn't do that with me. All I did was change the sewer pipe orders."

My hands dropped from her jacket. "What?"

"Can I sit down?"

"Yes, sure. But what were you and Frank doing with the sewer pipes?"

She sat, pulled the blanket in place, and took a long sip of brandy. "I work in the office of Solano Construction Company. We send in the pipe requisitions. Sewers take a lot of piping. One pipe has to fit into the next. If the size of an order is off, the pipes don't go together. If the pipes don't fit, the whole project stops."

I nodded.

"Frank wanted to delay the sewer construction. He paid me to alter the requisitions."

I stared at her in disbelief, yet knowing this was not a tale Patsy would invent. But the idea of Frank Goulet bribing Patsy to hold up the sewer system was almost too ludicrous to consider. I could imagine Frank spending money on a lot of things—ivory, netsukes, drugs—but not on obstructing sewers. "How did you do it?" I asked her.

"It was easy enough. I'd change a number 87 pipe to 78. Or I'd order casing that was too small, or too large. There's a lot that goes into building a sewer. It's not like the pipes under your kitchen sink, you know."

"How often did you do this?"

"Maybe once a month or so."

"Tell me how it worked, exactly. What did Frank do, and what did you do?"

She took another drink of brandy and leaned back, looking cool and in control again, as if the flush of panic just moments ago had never existed. "Frank called and arranged a meeting, like you said, in town or in the park. He didn't want to discuss anything on the phone. He'd ask what I could do at that time. I mean, we didn't order every item every week. I had to work with what I had. So I'd tell him. Then we'd discuss money."

"You bargained?"

"Well, sort of. I told Frank what it would be worth to me, and then he'd go away and think about it. He always agreed, but it took two or three days each time."

"Why the delay?"

Patsy half shrugged. "I guess he was cheap."

"But why did Frank want the sewer delayed?"

Patsy favored me with her normal expression of disinterest. "He never said."

"Didn't you ask?"

"No."

I believed her. Anyone else would have demanded an explanation, but Patsy wouldn't even have been curious. "Surely," I said, "you couldn't have gone on altering requisitions indefinitely."

"Frank knew that. He said eventually the taxpayers would get tired of paying more and more for a system that never neared completion. And if that didn't happen before the requisitions ran out, he'd think of something else. So far it hadn't been a problem."

"And Frank paid you each time?"

"Of course. I wouldn't have done it otherwise."

"How many orders did you change?"

"I don't know—seven, eight, something like that. It started a couple months after I got here, if that's what you want to know." She glanced toward the brandy bottle.

I refilled both our glasses, finishing off the bottle. "This is a big fraud. It must be costing the taxpayers hundreds of thousands of dollars. Aren't you worried?"

"It's only ripping off the government. Cost overruns. It happens all the time." She said it with the sureness of the sixties, but the caution of the intervening years was evident on her face.

"Who else knew about this?"

"No one, unless Frank told them."

"Not Paul?"

She shook her head.

"You didn't tell your own husband?"

"No. He was better off not knowing."

And Patsy was safer. Again, I was struck by her constant control. Patsy had no soft edges, no sides of her personality untended.

"Didn't Paul wonder where the extra money came from?"

"Maybe. I doubt it. Extra money is never the problem. And before you ask, Vejay, I didn't kill Frank. His death was a bummer for me. Paul and I will never make it just renting canoes."

Taking a final sip of brandy, I stood up, pulled on my slicker, and left.

I ran through the water to my pickup, then sat there until the engine warmed. I wanted to get out of the Fernandez' parking lot before Paul got back. At best he'd be furious that I'd sent him to

"I'm arresting you for grand theft." Sheriff Wescott stood behind his blue desk in his blue office. It was only seven-thirty but this part of the building was night-quiet. Lights in other offices were out and shadows pushed at the plexiglass office walls.

From the visitor's chair, I stared at him. I had ridden to Guerneville in the back of the patrol car, behind the wire mesh, in silence. The driver had been the same deputy I'd eluded earlier in the day. "Grand theft?" I asked.

"The Chinese ceremonial plates." Now Wescott sat down.

I waited.

"Martin Walucyk called me this afternoon. He reported a ransom contact from a youngish woman with long, irregularly cut, brown hair, wearing jeans and a yellow crewneck sweater." He eyed my clothes; I hadn't been home to change. "Driving a brown pickup truck."

I sat, too stunned to speak. I really didn't expect Walucyk to call the sheriff. I didn't think he'd leave his dining room.

"That's ridiculous," I said. My voice sounded weak.

"Walucyk will identify you."

"Of course, he'll do that. I'm not denying I was there." That came out better.

"Then you're admitting to perpetrating the theft along with Goulet."

"Certainly not."

"Come on now, Miss Haskell. We've got evidence."

Looking at Wescott, I realized that his threats and wheedling in the past had been of an altogether different class of maneuver. When he sat in my living room drinking my coffee and eating my toast, he assumed I was concealing some interesting but basically trivial fact. He had made a show of telling me, but he hadn't seriously considered me a suspect. Now he stared with disgust. It was no longer "Vejay" but "Miss Haskell." Now I was a suspect, and worse yet, one who had made a fool of him.

"You don't have evidence because there is none," I said.

"Tell that to Walucyk."

"I told Walucyk I was a writer. He chose to think I was connected with the thief. That misconception encouraged him to answer my questions. I wasn't about to disabuse him."

"You didn't 'disabuse' him because you were there to arrange the ransom. You can help yourself by telling me where those plates are before I have to go to the trouble of getting a search warrant."

Jesus! A search warrant! The Chinese plate was still on my mantel.

"What are you going to search?" I demanded. "You've already been through virtually every room in my house, and in my garage. From what Walucyk told me those plates are big and they oxidize quickly. They're not things you plunk under the sink." I leaned back in my chair, hoping that made me look more assured. "I assume you've searched Frank's Place and his apartment."

He nodded.

"Do you really think if I were involved in a three-hundred-thousand-dollar theft, I would come barrelling in here demanding you check out Frank for drugs? Do you think I would irritate every one of my friends hassling them about Frank? Do you think I would drive to Walucyk's house in my own truck, in"—I eyed my sweater and jeans—"this clever disguise?"

"You knew where Walucyk lived."

"His address was in the paper."

"You connected the theft to Goulet."

"For obvious reasons. They are the two big crimes of the year here."

"There are plenty of crimes that are unrelated. Now how exactly did you figure Goulet for this one?"

I realized Frank took the plates because I found the one in his secret room. I could hardly admit that. But I couldn't refuse to answer either, not with a search warrant threatened.

I took a breath. "It was something Madge Oombs told me. You remember I mentioned talking to her?"

"Go on."

"Well, I ran into her again, quite accidentally, in the supermarket, and more to fill the time till she could get rid of me than anything else, she told me a tale she had related to Frank when he first came here, about a Japanese bronze buddha." I related the story to him.

"So?"

"At the time I didn't think anything of it, either.

But then I realized it was an odd thing to tell
Frank. Frank was a bartender. He had some interest in ivory and figurines, but not in bronze. Why
did Madge tell him that? Madge isn't a chatterer.
She wouldn't have been filling time with him like
she was with me. There had to have been a reason.
Something Frank said had to have occasioned the
story. So, I figured Frank must have been asking
about bronze, oriental bronze. And that led me to
the Chinese bronze plates."

I waited, hardly breathing. Wescott didn't say
anything. He couldn't decide.

"According to Chris Fortimiglio," I added,
"Frank had a habit of researching areas of art that
interested him. You could ask Madge what Frank
said."

"I doubt she'd remember after two years."

"You could ask."

He nodded, a little rocking motion with his
head.

I tried to keep the show of relief off my face. I
wasn't in the clear yet. The plate was still on the
mantel. Frank's financial records were in my
drawer.

"Where have you been today?" Wescott asked.

I laughed. "At Walucyk's."

"You left there at one thirty-seven."

I laughed again, this time forced. "I came home
the long way. I was afraid Walucyk might call the
highway patrol and I didn't want to be stopped on
the Golden Gate Bridge."

"Six hours," he said. "You must have gone
through San Jose."

"And I haven't had dinner yet. It is eight

o'clock." I waited, unsure whether I could really leave.

Wescott looked unsure too. "I don't have enough to hold you," he said finally. He didn't add that he would be watching me. I didn't need to be told. "The deputy will drive you home."

"Thanks, but as long as I'm in Guerneville, I think I'll eat here. I can always find a ride home."

Even if I had to walk all six miles in the rain, with the flood water inching toward North Bank Road, I wasn't going to let another sheriff near my living room and the Chinese plate.

I was too unnerved to be hungry when I left the Sheriff's Department, but I decided I'd better do as I said and have dinner in Guerneville before going home.

The bakery, the drugstore, the normal places I grabbed something to eat, were closed. The only place still open was The Pines, a restaurant with tablecloths. It was more formal than I had in mind, more so than I was dressed for, and likely to cost more than I wanted to pay. The hostess, apparently sharing my assessment, sat me at a table next to the kitchen door.

It seemed like days since I'd left Walucyk's with the knowledge that Frank had a partner. And Patsy had insisted that she was not that person.

There was no reason not to believe Patsy's story. But Frank as a preservationist? Ned had said Frank was very anti-growth. I'd discounted Ned's view, colored as it was by his own prejudices. But Frank had been paying Patsy to sabotage the sewer. What would he have gained? Frank rarely left his bar. He had never, to my knowledge, gone to the town beach. He got seasick in a canoe. Keeping Henderson unspoiled wouldn't have mattered to him. More residents would have meant a better trade at the Place. And even if that business were not his main interest, any growth in population would have been primarily summer people, who, in winter, would have left empty homes waiting to be burglarized.

It didn't make sense.

My salmon arrived. My appetite rebounded. I ate thoughtlessly, staring at the other diners. Despite the weather, and the impending flood, the restaurant was crowded. Whole families were grouped around big tables in the center of the room. Couples sat by the windows. At a corner table, by the window, was Skip Bollo, alone.

Frank had asked Skip about buying a restaurant. That had been only a month ago. Why would he seek another business if he were against growth? He would not want fewer but more people in the area if he were establishing a new restaurant.

I tried some salad. That was good, too.

Why would Frank try to buy a business when he, of all people, knew that the sewer would be delayed indefinitely and he would never be able to open that restaurant?

When I talked with Skip in his office that night, we discussed restaurants on the river. I'd been thinking about moving marijuana from the restaurant, by canoe, to Frank's trap door. Rather than being interested in a restaurant, per se, Frank might have merely sought a dwelling on the riverbank.

Taking a final large bite of salmon, I got up and made my way to Skip's table.

As he recognized me approaching, Skip sighed.

I sat down across from him. "I'll only be a minute."

He put down his fork and waited.

"Do you remember telling me Frank asked you about restaurants for sale? When was that?"

"A month and a half, maybe two months ago. Why?"

"Was he only interested in restaurants?"

"Restaurants or stores that could be converted to restaurants, like butcher shops or groceries."

"Was it just places along the river?"

Skip smacked both hands down on the table. "Look, Vejay, you used to be a nice enough young woman, but you're getting to be a pest. I can't eat breakfast out without being observed by you. I can't dine out without you barging in. And what kind of foolish questions are you asking me? 'Was it only restaurants by the river?' This is the 'Russian River Resort Area.' The attraction here is the river. Restaurants are built by the river, where people can enjoy it. People don't build their restaurants on the side of the hill, so that they are hard to find, so that there's no parking, so that mudslides cut off access to them half the year."

"But did Frank specify he wanted a place on the river?" I insisted.

"I don't know, Vejay. I can't remember every word of a conversation that took place months ago. It probably never came up. Now will you go away?"

I wanted to apologize for making such a nuisance of myself, but I couldn't. I wanted to finish my dinner, but I didn't do that either. I paid the bill and left.

It was still raining. I considered beginning the six-mile walk. I toyed with the idea of going back to the sheriff's department and asking for a ride. Instead, I opted for stationing myself on the corner by the traffic light and hoping that someone I knew would come along. I stood under the street-light and pulled off the hood of my slicker so all my friends (what friends I had left) could see who I was. The rain ran down my hair, down my neck. The strong wind off the Pacific streaked my cheeks.

Still, it wasn't long before Carlo Fortimiglio's battered old Chevy pickup pulled over to the curb.

"What are you doing here, Vejay?" Rosa called out the window. She was leaning across Chris.

"Hoping someone would drive me home."

"Well, get in."

"Where?" I said, peering into the well-occupied cab.

"Chris can ride in the back," Rosa offered.

"He'll be soaked."

"He can get under the tarpaulin."

"Or you can sit on my lap," Chris said to me, as he opened the door and offered me a hand up.

Used to my own little pickup cab, I was sur-prised at how roomy the old American ones were. Had Rosa and Carlo been thinner, and Chris smaller in general, all of us might have fit on the seat. Even now, perched on Chris's lap, I had room for my legs and only had to stoop my head a little.

"What are you doing in Guerneville?" I asked before they could question me.

"Carlo had to take a last load of sand to bag around the Simpson house," Rosa said. "I came

llong and brought a couple pots of spaghetti up to
he shelter."

"That was nice of you."

"Well, we had it. And when it floods, some of
he new people leave their houses in such a hurry
hey don't think to bring food."

"The river rises much faster than you new folks
expect," Chris said to me. "City people assume it
ust eases over the banks. They don't understand
hat the crest starts upriver and comes down like a
wave. One minute a house on the bank is dry and
he next, as quick as that, it's under water. Or
washed away."

"Chris, Chris," Rosa cried, "no need to scare
Vejay." To me, she added, "You don't have to
worry. Your house is high up. The water never
reaches it."

I smiled halfheartedly. But in the dark cab that
made no difference. For lack of anything better to
say, I said, "I guess you've all had a hard day."

"Tomorrow's another long one," Chris said.
"We've got another place west of town that needs
work. And there are always emergencies right before the flood."

The truck bounced in a pothole. My head hit
the roof.

"You okay, Vejay?"

"Yes. It's only my head, Chris."

He laughed.

"Do you remember telling me about Frank collecting oriental art?" I asked.

"Oh, yes."

"Did he ever mention knowing other collectors?"

Chris was silent a moment, tapping a finger on my shoulder in thought. "No."

"He never went to art sales, or museum openings?"

"I don't think so, Vejay. He bought his stuff overseas. And when he sold it he was in a rush for money. Besides, he really wasn't the arty type. Why are you asking that?"

"Mmm," Rosa added her curiosity to Chris's. Carlo, as usual, drove in silence.

"I'm just trying to figure Frank out. I remember you saying, Chris, that he hated to be cheated. He resented it more than most men."

"That's true."

"And Ned told me he waited a year to get even with a guy who'd beaten him in the park."

"Oh, no," Rosa said.

"No, Ma, Frank was like that. You just didn't see that side."

"Oh, Chris, I just can't—"

"Here you are, Vejay." Carlo stopped the truck in my driveway. "Better get your kerosene lamp ready before the power goes out."

"I would have forgotten. Thanks, Carlo." I clambered down off Chris's lap and out of the truck.

Amidst my thanks and their offers of meals when the power went out, they left. I started up my fifty-two steps, past my garage that had been broken into and not repaired, to do something about the Chinese plate that had probably caused Frank's death.

CHAPTER
20

I planned to spend the rest of the evening puzzling out what I had learned, finding among those facts and speculations real evidence of Frank's killer. I settled in the tub, turned my thoughts to the sewer project, and suddenly realized that I had come within half an inch of drowning. I'd fallen asleep in the tub. After that, I roused myself long enough to get into bed, stopping only to put the incriminating Chinese dish in a paper bag on top of my purse. I didn't have a plan for it, but at least it was no longer in plain sight.

In the morning I raced from the bedroom to the kitchen, gulping coffee, while I brushed my "irregularly cut" hair and applied the minimum amount of make-up necessary to make me look alive. Rain hit the windows. The house was icy, but I was too rushed to do more than notice. My suspension from work was over, and as usual, I was nearly late.

Had I speculated about how Mr. Bobbs would greet my return, I would have guessed he'd be hidden away in his office, and a brief, very formal note would be in my message slot. And so it was. I read it amidst the greetings of my fellow meter readers, their complaints about the mud, the rain, and the angry customers whose power had already gone out, and the tale of several old-time custom-

ers who knew the day their meters should have
been read and were enraged at my not being there.

The route I had started on Tuesday was still not
completed. I signed out truck twelve (with which I
was very familiar) and drove the couple of blocks
into town. The incriminating paper bag holding
the Chinese plate was stashed under the seat. I still
had no plans for it, but removing it from my house
seemed a step in the right direction.

The rain, the mudslides, and the washed-out
roads all over the hillside made me glad to be doing the flat, paved commercial section of the route.
Afterwards there would be only one hillside area
left. And that included Walucyk's summer house.

On a normal day the town route would be
pleasant. The meters would be accessible, the merchants friendly, and there would be no dogs likely
to snarl at me. I'd walk along the street chatting
with shoppers, enjoying the town. But with the
river expected to flood at any moment, the street
was deserted. Rain had speckled the meter covers,
making it hard to see the dials inside. I couldn't
take the route book out of the truck as I usually
did; I had to leave it inside and, between each
reading, come back to record the usage. I dragged
the truck from meter to meter. Ned Jacobs drove
by, pausing to announce that he was headed to the
supermarket. Madge Oombs stood in front of her
shop, nailing the shutters down. The rain gave her
an excuse, if she needed it, not to speak.

By eleven, this section of the route was done. I
was starved. I bought a hamburger and a Coke
and sat in the truck to do the thinking I'd planned
for last night.

I had Frank's financial records at home. He had

not ordered supplies since he'd stolen the Chinese plates. Was he planning to leave town? Take his two hundred thousand dollars and disappear? If he did this, Frank would have been abandoning a good business, one he had apparently enjoyed. Why wouldn't he have planned to hide the money and keep the Place? He could have had some great vacations on half of four hundred thousand dollars.

Or the full four hundred thousand dollars!

Had Frank planned to take the entire ransom and leave his partner with nothing but the sheriff? That would certainly explain why he was killed.

Or had he suspected that it would be too dangerous to stay in town? Had he figured that, given time, the theft of the plates, the ransom calls, the other burglaries, would all inevitably be traced back to him?

But why had he asked Skip Bollo about buying another restaurant? Obviously he had no intention of doing so. Did he want to convince Skip he was staying in town? There would have been only one reason for that.

Was Skip, then, Frank's partner? Was it Skip that Frank planned to leave standing amidst the remains of the theft when the sheriff arrived? I couldn't imagine Skip Bollo breaking into a house. And, assuming that the burglaries corresponded to Frank's contacts with Patsy, they happened approximately once per month. I doubted whether either partner's share would be more than a couple of hundred dollars. Frank's must have barely paid Patsy.

Then, was Patsy the only person who truly benefited from the burglaries?

Suddenly, the two or three days necessary to confirm the agreement with Patsy became reasonable. It was not Frank, who was uninterested in preserving the area, who paid Patsy. Frank was the intermediary. His partner, someone concerned with delaying the sewer, was the one who sent money to Patsy.

Had the burglaries themselves been set up for the purpose of financing the sewer sabotage?

Besides Skip, who would benefit from delaying the sewer? Madge? Ned? The Fortimiglios? Either monetarily, or from the preservation of the area, all of them would have something to gain.

I sighed and finished my Coke.

Perhaps, if I looked at the problem from a more practical point . . . In planning the burglaries, who would know which houses to hit? Again, anyone. I needed to see Walucyk's house to see how desirable it looked from the outside. If it was new, expensive, likely to contain fenceable goods, then it wouldn't require any expertise to select it. Conversely then, if it was uninviting, the only way Frank's partner would have been alerted to the treasure within was if he or she had already been inside the house.

I drove the truck through town and up the hillside road. The pavement had been narrowed to one lane by intermittent slides. I pulled the truck in between the mounds of dirt, waiting for oncoming vehicles to pass, and then went on. Parking at the top of the hill, I worked my way down, dragging the truck from house to house, coming back after each foray through a muddy drive or sodden yard. I saved Walucyk's for last, so I wouldn't

ave any more offended customers to complain
at their meters had been overlooked.

From the outside, Walucyk's house bore no re-
mblance to his luxurious San Francisco Victo-
an home. The yard was overgrown; it looked like
alucyk didn't hire a gardener. The house itself
as no bigger than mine, and the wood was
ainted green rather than stained and varnished
ke the newer and more expensive homes. Drapes
overed the front window. From the street there
as no way of telling what was inside. It was not
house that would catch a burglar's eye.

I went around the back to the meter, which, as
ith many older homes, was on the porch. That
as lucky for me—it meant I had a key.

I paused long enough outside the door to peer
, but nothing more than the meter and a folded
eck chair was visible on the little porch. I let my-
lf in and jotted down the usage figures.

No one who had not been inside the house
ould have known that there was anything valu-
ple here. But who would have reason to be here?
Walucyk said he did not socialize in Henderson.
Nothing had been built, nothing repaired. He cer-
inly hadn't hired a local person to do yardwork.
lad Madge Oombs made a sale or bought some
inor piece of Walucyk's collection? It was hard
o imagine any one item that could grace both
alucyk's home and Madge's shop. Had Skip
een through the house before Walucyk bought it
nd noted the display cases? Even if he had, he
ould not have known what Walucyk planned to
eep in them. As for Ned Jacobs, or Paul, Patsy, or
he Fortimiglios, I couldn't imagine Walucyk both-

ering to speak to them, much less have them in hi
house.

There was nothing to do but go inside.

I tried my key in the lock on the door. I wasn'
surprised when it didn't fit. We meter readers wer
bonded; PG&E went to a lot of trouble to assur
customers their readers were honest. But that di
not inspire many people into giving us a key t
their homes. Meters were usually on porches, no
in bedrooms.

If I intended to see the inside of Walucyk'
house, I'd have to break in. With a start, I realize
how naturally the thought came to me—me, wh
only a week before had been a law-abiding
woman.

Pushing self-assessment aside, I stared at th
back door. It had a two-foot square window, bi
enough for me to hoist myself through. But th
moment I'd break the glass, alarms would rin
from here to Guerneville.

Gusts of wind shook the flimsy walls of th
porch; the glass in the outside door rattled. Th
sky was dark as dusk though it was still afternoon
There were no squares of yellow in the distance
no warm lights showing through the trees. N
lights were on in the other houses.

I looked closer at Walucyk's electricity meter
the five dials stared back. All five were motionless
Walucyk said he had display cases inside. If h
visited on weekends he would have left his refrigerator on. It would need power. His meter dial
should have been moving. I now wished that I ha
read the other meters on the hillside more carefully. Were they running, or was the power off on
this side of town? Or all over town?

If Walucyk's power was off, the alarm system would be dead. I'd have to chance it. Picking up the deck chair, I broke the window.

There was no bell, no loud buzzing, nothing here to suggest the alarm had sounded. But still, it could be one of those that alerted only the sheriff.

Quickly, I hoisted myself through the window and into the kitchen. To my right was the dining room—small, but expensively decorated in old rough oak and thick oriental carpets.

I hurried into the living room. It was similar to the room I'd seen in Walucyk's Victorian. Being much smaller, it had only one oriental carpet, one uncomfortable-looking brocade sofa, two matching chairs, and three display cases (one on the front wall and two on the interior wall across from it).

The case on the front wall, the one that had housed the Chinese plates, was empty, the scratches from its forced entry still visible.

I stood absolutely still and listened, but there was no noise outside other than the sound of trees scraping against the house and the rain pelting the windows. No sirens, no tires squealing.

Across from the empty display case, on the interior wall, was a second case that held a group of small silk Chinese screens. The case had not been touched. And apparently Walucyk had not felt it worthwhile to remove the collection after the theft of the plates.

The third and last case contained Japanese netsukes of animals and minuscule people. I stooped over, surveying the collection: an ivory puppy wrapped around a ball, the whole thing no more than two inches tall; a pile of monkeys with tails and legs intertwined. The little figures were grouped casually, but one stood apart. It was a netsuke of three old women standing back to back, and one of the women had gold teeth. Frank's netsuke! The netsuke he sold for a tenth of its value!

Frank, who hated to be taken, had been taken by Walucyk.

I could picture Frank selling the netsuke to Walucyk and imagine Walucyk's smug pleasure in telling Frank its true value. Frank had waited a year to get even with the man in the park. It took him more than two years to get back at Walucyk.

I realized now that I had been viewing the entire burglary scheme backwards. Frank and his partner did not come across the plates in the course of housebreaking. It was the other way around. Frank's need for revenge prompted the burglaries.

Frank must have sold the netsuke to Walucyk in San Francisco. I could picture Walucyk telling Frank about his weekend house, just as he told me. I could imagine him showing Frank his other collections, those collections he was so proud of that he insisted that I, whom he assumed to be a thief, view them. Frank would have seen the Chinese plates there. And there, he would have sworn to get revenge.

The desire for revenge must have given birth to Frank's move to Henderson. He came here, found a partner (he'd have to have a partner to do the actual burglaries), and bought the Place for its secret room.

No wonder Frank had asked Madge Oombs about oriental bronze right after he moved here. It must have been on his mind constantly then.

Frank was good at research. He would have read the news accounts of Walucyk, the collector, just as I did. He would have noted Professor Everson's attempt to buy the plates from Walucyk. How Frank must have enjoyed calling and pretending to be Smithson, leading Walucyk on, and using his own arrogance to convince him to move the plates to Henderson. How he must have loved making the ransom calls and then raising the price. Frank was the one person who wouldn't have cared if the plates were never fenced. It wasn't money he wanted. If Walucyk agreed to the four-hundred-thousand dollar demand, would Frank have raised it to five? Would Frank ever return the plates to Walucyk?

Looking back at the little figures in Frank's netsuke, I was surprised that Frank resisted taking it. But Frank, of course, was not the actual burglar. Frank and his red sports car were at the Place, a clear alibi.

So then the accomplice, who must have been there listening to Frank raise the ransom price, must have killed him.

I took one last look at the netsuke. Even in the dim light of the house its gold teeth glistened.

I hurried out the back door, leaving it banging in the wind and rain, and ran up the incline toward my truck. In spite of the rain, something about the truck looked odd. I was still a few feet away when I discovered what it was.

The left front window had been smashed.

I stood, staring at my truck. The window on the driver's side was broken. Glass shards had fallen on the seat and the floor. Rain, heavier still now, was coming in through the broken window.

How was I going to explain this to Mr. Bobbs? While I had been on my PG&E route, housebreaking, someone smashed my truck window. Just like someone took an axe to my pickup engine. It was beginning to sound ridiculous.

Who would vandalize a PG&E truck? People cheated on their usage, people complained about rate increases, but no one broke windows on our trucks. Amongst the corporate dollar-gobblers, we were mere nibblers. No one felt that strongly about PG&E.

I reached under the seat for the whisk brush. As I cleared away the glass, the rain pelted against my back.

Replacing the brush, I noticed the empty passenger seat. My route book was gone! Frantically, I searched the truck, but the Chinese plate in its brown paper bag was still safe under the seat. Only the route book was missing.

Nothing could be so dull or useless to anyone else as a utility route book. Yet someone had stolen it. Someone had taken the chance of breaking into my truck, right here on the street, for the purpose of taking my route book.

I climbed into the truck. The seat was wet. The rain blew through the window and smacked against my face. I made a U-turn and stopped the truck, good-window side to the rain.

What could anyone—not just anyone—what could Frank Goulet's killer want with my route book?

This day's route, the remainder of the one I had been on Tuesday, included the town and the commercial routes on both sides of the river all the way to the west bridge. Did he, or she, know that? It would be easy enough to find out. Anyone could call the office and ask when their meter would be read. So, what did Frank's killer need from this particular route book?

I sat back, considering Frank's killer.

Had Frank's killer and partner been privy to the plan to steal Walucyk's Chinese plates when they set up the burglary operation? I doubted it. No one but Frank would take the risks involved to steal a set of plates too distinctive to fence, and then agree to toy with the one person who would pay money to get them back. A partner might steal them for ransom, but he would never raise the price one hundred thousand dollars above their value (above what the insurance would reimburse) just so Frank could enjoy his revenge. Frank apparently was willing to chance pushing Walucyk to the point where he would not or could not pay, but no partner would have acquiesced.

More likely, the partner had joined a simple, relatively safe burglary operation. It had earned him a little extra money, enough to keep the sewer system from completion.

But how did they know which places (other than Walucyk's) to burgle? Even a simple casing of a house required more than driving by in second gear. It meant parking, getting out, checking on means of entry, on neighbors, on alarms. Who could do that time after time without drawing attention?

The most likely suspect, the one with a truck that could be parked for an hour without raising questions was, alas, me. My PG&E truck was a common sight; it had reason to be anywhere. No one noticed me. The only people who recalled seeing me were the old people across from Frank's Monday. Monday! And then I hadn't been working. I wasn't driving the PG&E truck. The old people recalled seeing me at Frank's Place Monday because I had driven my own pickup, which would not normally be there at that time of day. They remembered seeing Chris for the same reason. But the Chinese Laundry truck, which they saw every day, made no impression on them at all. They never mentioned that to the sheriff.

Suddenly, it all fell together. There was only one other truck in town that could be anywhere with good reason; one truck that could be parked by the riverbank or by Frank's without causing any notice. The owner of that truck could easily have business there. For Frank's killer, the risks in burglarizing houses would be worthwhile if he earned enough to stop the sewer and the urbanization of Henderson. Even with the money from the burglaries, it still might take a few days to get the cash to give to Frank for Patsy—thus the delay she complained of.

I knew who the killer was. It only made me feel sad. Had I thought about it before, I would have realized there was no way not to be distressed, no matter who the killer was. My discovery would ruin our community. The Henderson of Ned's childhood vacations would be broken apart, the safety and the magic gone forever. It had been inevitable since Frank's death, actually since the first burglary. I wished Frank had never come to Henderson. I wished I could forget about Frank and let the murderer go. But I, of all people, had no choice.

The sheriff was concentrating on me. In his eyes, I had motive, opportunity, and possible connections in San Francisco to fence the stolen items. I had worked in the city at twice my present salary long enough to develop expensive tastes. Once the sheriff discovered, as he inevitably would, that I had searched Frank's Place and had possession of the Chinese devotional plate . . .

Still, I didn't steal my own route book. But in the face of the potential evidence against me, I doubted if I could convince Wescott even of that.

Although I knew the identity of the killer, I needed to find him quickly, before the flood waters burst through town and washed away any evidence of my route book or the Chinese plate. I needed to find out why he took the route book. And I needed to get to him before he made use of it.

I put the truck in first gear and drove slowly along the hilly lanes. The wind was gusty. Rain spit in through the broken window. Oil lamps flickered in a few houses. Those with shutters folded them closed over the windows. Smoke pouring thick from chimneys mixed with the rain to form a gray paste between the land and what light there was left in the sky. I turned on the headlights.

I discovered the Chinese plate because of Frank's electricity usage. His increased usage was necessary to run the space heaters and the dehumidifier he needed to preserve the bronze finish of the plates. The plates were no longer in Frank's Place. Frank's Place had been ransacked after I was there, by someone looking for those plates. It couldn't have been Martin Walucyk. He didn't know Frank's name, much less where he worked. It must have been Frank's partner.

And by the time he searched the Place, the plates were gone. Only two people knew the plates were hidden at Frank's. The killer was looking for them. So Frank must have been the one who had moved them in the first place, to hide them from his partner, to keep his partner from contacting Walucyk himself and arranging his own deal for the plates. But where had Frank taken them?

I slammed on the brakes. I wasn't watching the road. Ahead was a mudslide. I backed into a driveway and turned around. Frank hadn't been out of town in a month, so he told me. As far as I knew he had been at Frank's Place every day, even Sundays. So, wherever he took the plates, it had to be local. And it had to be a place where he could plug in his dehumidifier and heaters, someplace using electricity.

But why, then didn't he take the dehumidifier and the heaters? They were still in the secret room

beneath the Place. Did he load the plates into his
sports car and have no room left for the bulky
heaters? Was he murdered before he could make a
second trip to his new hiding place?

Frank had been asking about restaurants for
sale, but he hadn't actually bought any other
property. He would hardly have called PG&E for
a hookup on property he didn't own. So what I
was looking for was a place that wasn't listed in
the route book but was using electricity. An illegal
hookup. And that's what the killer was doing.
Since he had the route book, he could skip any
place listed in it. He had a big advantage.

I thought back over the portion of the route I
just completed, trying to recall empty houses.
There were plenty this time of year. But Frank
would have needed someplace where he'd be sure
no owner would turn up unexpectedly, someplace
that was empty and would be for a long time. And
it would have to have decent enough wiring for an
electrical hookup, wiring able to support two
heaters and a dehumidifier. No old house would
have that. I'd blown a fuse in my own house using
a heater and the hair dryer at the same time. What
Frank needed was commercial wiring.

A restaurant. Frank had asked Skip Bollo about
restaurants for sale. As Skip said, restaurants in
the Russian River Resort Area were on the river.
My route book covered the roads by the river.
That was the reason Frank's killer needed to have
my route book today. As Chris said last night, the
river would rise quickly, higher than the new people—like me and Frank—would expect. It would
invade the lower buildings on the riverbank. It
would knock down walls and wash away every-

thing inside. It would rush into Frank's new hiding place and sweep away the Chinese plates.

The water already covered the road. The killer didn't have much time. If he did get the Chinese plates out, this would be an ideal time to dispose of them, while everyone else was preoccupied with the flood. No one would notice if he was not around. He could drive to San Francisco with the plates and be back without anyone realizing he'd been gone.

I pictured the route along the river as it had been last month when I walked it. Mentally I walked from building to building, allowing myself no "fast forward" in my vision. There were numerous houses, and many motels and businesses closed for the winter that would reopen soon, too soon for Frank. Those were places whose owners would come up to assess the damage as soon as the flood waters receded. Frank needed a place no one would check.

There were three deserted commercial buildings at the west end of town. I started the engine and followed North Bank Road to the nearest, a weather-worn old place that might once have been a café. Its white shingles had turned gray-brown with years of exposure and neglect. Its porch swayed precariously over the river. Now, as I pulled to a stop in front, I could see the water lapping over the porch.

The building had been empty as long as I had been living here, and from everything I had heard, even years before that. As I made my way through the weeds toward the door, I could see a line around the side halfway up the windows—the

highwater mark from the last flood eight years
ago.

I followed the drop line to the weatherhead. The
wires were tied around the pole, their raw ends
flapping in the wind. There was no power on in
here.

I walked back to the truck, irrationally relieved
at having the confrontation postponed.

The second building, deserted even longer than
the first, was already a foot under water. No one
was around. No drop line even left the main line. I
drove on.

The water crested the bank. Across the river, I
could hear sirens. Water flowed onto the road. I
slowed as the road dipped and the truck wheels
went into the water. From either side of the road
redwood branches formed a dark green canopy,
alternately sheltering my truck and deluging it
with water. The last building, once a sandwich
shop, was ahead. The killer's truck was parked
outside. There had been no attempt to hide it. Had
I been passing, I would have thought nothing of it.
I pulled the truck in front, blocking its exit.

Automatically, I looked up for the drop line. It
came in from the street, attached to the
weatherhead. If I checked the meter, I would find
it bypassed. I had found Frank's illegal hookup.

I opened the truck door and pushed hard
against the wind to keep it from slamming back
into me as I climbed out. It banged shut, but the
noise wouldn't be heard above the battering of
branches against the building, or the clamor of debris hitting the deck pilings.

The water washed over the deck. It would be at
least a foot deep inside the building.

I passed his truck. In the back, piled unceremoniously, were eight boxes. The small plate was still stashed in my truck. That left only one still inside the building.

I wished . . . I pushed open the door.

Carlo Fortimiglio was holding the box in those strong arms that compensated for his injured leg. The box was large, wooden; it must have held one of the biggest plates. Looking at me, he shifted it to one arm, holding it as easily as he would one of his grandchildren.

"I'm sorry, Carlo," I said. With the rain pounding on the roof and the branches hitting against the wall, I didn't think my voice was loud enough to carry across the room. But Carlo nodded. He seemed to be deciding.

He beckoned me closer. The water was almost up to my knees. I clung to the doorjamb, then to the door, and let it open inward.

Carlo stood halfway across the room.

"This is as close as I can come," I said. Carlo had killed Frank. If he killed me, he'd be free. But he was Carlo—Carlo who dug my pickup out of a mudslide when I first came up here, Carlo who ladled the clam sauce onto Rosa's fettucini. Carlo who killed Frank.

"I know," I said. "Was it only for money to delay the sewer construction, to save your family's —?"

"To keep the fish, the town, for us. Yes." He stood braced against the wall, holding the box easily in his left arm. Suddenly the wind was calm, the room quiet. "But I didn't have a choice. Years, maybe ten years ago, there was a bad spell. I hit—burgled—some houses. I stashed away a little money. Chris let it slip. The boys in the Navy, they drink, they say things they shouldn't."

"Chris told Frank, and Frank threatened to go to the sheriff unless you burgled houses for him?"

"Yes, that. And he took my money, for his down payment. He said he'd pay it back." Carlo made a sound between crying and laughing. The wind grew stronger, but still I had no trouble hearing him.

Carlo took a step toward me. "But I don't excuse myself. I didn't argue. Why should I? We didn't steal from local people, only summer people. They could afford it. They have insurance. I didn't take too much. Maybe I hit one house a month."

The stolen goods would have gone into Carlo's old truck, a common sight in town as he hauled wood, carted off debris, or repaired a deck. It was the truck no one would notice. With his injured leg, Carlo might be unsteady on a rolling boat, but as I watched him stand in the rising water, holding the box, there was no question he had well compensated for it on land.

"Frank chose the house you took the plates from," I prompted.

He looked down at the box. Again, he stepped closer, within a foot of me. "I figured it was just another hit. But later, the more I thought about it, how did Frank know to take the plates, the plates but not the little statues? How did he know who to call for ransom? How much to ask? Then I figured he had planned it all along. He made a fool of me.

"I told him—this is big stuff. He'll get the sheriff, and the state police, maybe the FBI after us. I old him—get rid of these." He stared down in atred at the box. "But Frank, he says I got no hoice. Then he calls the guy who owns them and ells him three hundred thousand dollars isn't nough money. He wants four hundred thousand lollars. I hear the guy argue. I hear him say he loesn't have it. When Frank gets off the phone he aughs. He says 'Maybe five hundred thousand.' I ell Frank he's crazy. There isn't going to be any ive hundred thousand dollars. No four hundred housand. No money. No money at all. All we're oing to get is the sheriff.

"Frank laughs. He says the sheriff won't find im. He can disappear like that." Carlo snapped is fingers. The box bounced in his arm.

"I shot him. I had to," he said so softly that I ould barely hear him. "He would have gone and eft me with no money, nothing but trouble."

"And you were going to call Walucyk and take he three hundred thousand dollars? And then vhen you looked for the plates they were gone?"

Carlo nodded, but I could see his mind was else-vhere.

"Yes. And now," Carlo said, "I'll go to jail. All he burglaries will be known. Everyone in town vill know I'm a thief. And the insurance compa-ies, they'll be after me; they'll take our house and he fishing boat. And lawyers . . ."

I could almost see him realizing that with me lead, no one would know. No police, insurance ompanies, lawyers.

Something smashed into the building. The box ame flying at me. I screamed, jumped, but it aught my shoulder and threw me back, down nto the water. I grabbed for the door, missed, and slid across the floor toward the deck, toward the swirling brown waters of the river. I grabbed for the doorjamb, where the back door to the deck had been. The whole building shook. Something else—big and heavy—smashed against the side of the room. The supports underneath me swayed. I clung to the wall, bracing my feet against the other side of the doorway, working them toward the inside of the wall. The water was swirling; it had gotten deeper in just those few moments. I braced my feet and grasped at the slippery doorjamb. Desperately, I looked back into the room.

Carlo was holding on to the front doorknob, blocking the way to the street. Even if I could get across the room, he could easily push me down into the water. I didn't know whether he had hurled the box at me, or if it had been thrown from his grasp by the movement of the building.

"Carlo, help me."

My hands were slipping. The water covered my thighs, smashing debris against me.

"Carlo!"

He looked at me. I couldn't read his expression.

He stretched away from the door and extended his arm. His hand was only a foot away. If I let go I could reach it. If he let go, he could send me into the river. I looked at his face again.

A branch hit my legs. My knees buckled. I grabbed for Carlo's hand.

Time seemed to stop the moment I touched Carlo's fingers. Nothing moved; neither he, nor I, nor the water. And then it started again. Carlo pulled me in. I caught the doorknob and clung, scrambling my feet under me.

The building was hit again. It didn't seem as

strong a shake as before. Maybe it was enough to knock Carlo's hands loose. Maybe the effort of pulling me in weakened him. Maybe.

His body swept across the room like a pillow in the water. For an instant it caught at the door-jamb, where I had held on, then passed right by me, into the river.

CHAPTER
22

I staggered out of the old sandwich shop to my truck. The small Chinese plate was still under the seat. Not pausing to see how badly oxidized its finish had gotten, I stuck it in the back of Carlo's truck, among the others. One plate was at the bottom of the river, the other nine were in bad shape. Even dead, Frank Goulet had gotten his revenge.

The water had already seeped into the cab of my truck. I was lucky to get the engine started, luckier yet to get through on North Bank Road. From there, I headed over to the sheriff's department.

The session with Sheriff Wescott took hours. He sent one deputy out to get me cocoa and offered to have another fetch me dry clothes. The closest he came to admitting he had erred in suspecting me of murdering Frank Goulet was to smile and say, "So you two were really just friends, huh?" Then he reminded me that each time he talked to me he'd been sure I was withholding something. And since there were things I still couldn't tell him about (like breaking into Frank's Place, stealing the PG&E truck to get there, or keeping the Chinese plate on my mantel overnight) there was nothing more to say.

It had been raining all night, and then, as if the rain had been part of a movie and we were walk-

ing out of the theater, it stopped. By morning the
sun was out, bright. The river, of course, continued to flood, but somehow, in the sun, it seemed
more entertaining than ominous.

I was told that when it floods, all the towns-
people wade down to the donut shop, buy crullers
and coffee, and walk out to the main bridge—
forty some feet above the riverbed—to watch the
flood waters rush under them. They look at the
markers, watch debris float by, and reminisce
about the flood of '64 or '47. It's a party, a cele-
bration of surviving another bout with nature. By
noon, someone always just happens to have found
a bottle of champagne. A grocery owner, whose
stock is going to be flooded anyway, provides a
few more.

I went down to the bridge. But there was no
party. People were there, crowding both sides, but
no one was laughing. Few even seemed to be talking. When I arrived, the people nearest me—the
Greshams, who owned the hardware store—either
didn't recognize me or turned away. I moved on,
nearer the center. No one said anything. They
would know by now that Carlo was dead, that
Carlo had killed Frank, and that I had been the
one to expose Carlo.

At the far end of the bridge I spotted Paul and
Patsy Fernandez, listening to a man who had his
back to me. They looked at each other, then
turned and hurried off the bridge in the direction
of their boat rental. They would disappear; I knew
that. They would take advantage of the commo-
tion as Carlo might have. They would turn up
somewhere else, with different names, waiting on
tables or renting canoes.

Skip Bollo was on the other side of the road-way, staring down at the brown water, watching the town—as it had been—flow under the bridge.

I stopped beside Ned Jacobs, wondering if he, too, would unconsciously blame me for Carlo, for the town.

But he didn't. He didn't speak. He just rested a hand on my shoulder.

I leaned against him, surprised by my need for support from a friend, after the long night hours with the sheriff.

"There was no way I couldn't tell the sheriff," I said. "I didn't want to. Carlo saved me. He pulled me back."

Ned firmed the arm around my shoulder. "You wouldn't have been there but for him, Vejay."

"Maybe they won't connect all the burglaries to him. I mean, who knows? Maybe the insurance companies won't bother. Martin Walucyk will have nine of his ten plates. It's his own fault for bringing them up here. He . . ." I realized I was crying.

I remembered the last time I had cried, sitting at the table in Frank's Place after talking to Sheriff Wescott. Rosa had come over, touched my arm, taken me home to dinner. Halfway across the bridge I saw her and Chris. Our eyes met. She turned away.